# COWBOY
## LEGACY

### SHIPMENT 1

*Courted by the Cowboy* by Sasha Summers
*A Valentine for the Cowboy* by Rebecca Winters
*The Maverick's Bridal Bargain* by Christy Jeffries
*A Baby for the Deputy* by Cathy McDavid
*Safe in the Lawman's Arms* by Patricia Johns
*The Rancher and the Baby* by Marie Ferrarella

### SHIPMENT 2

*Cowboy Doctor* by Rebecca Winters
*Rodeo Rancher* by Mary Sullivan
*The Cowboy Takes a Wife* by Trish Milburn
*A Baby for the Sheriff* by Mary Leo
*The Kentucky Cowboy's Baby* by Heidi Hormel
*Her Cowboy Lawman* by Pamela Britton

### SHIPMENT 3

*A Texas Soldier's Family* by Cathy Gillen Thacker
*A Baby on His Doorstep* by Roz Denny Fox
*The Rancher's Surprise Baby* by Trish Milburn
*A Cowboy to Call Daddy* by Sasha Summers
*Made for the Rancher* by Rebecca Winters
*The Rancher's Baby Proposal* by Barbara White Daille
*The Cowboy and the Baby* by Marie Ferrarella

### SHIPMENT 4

*Her Stubborn Cowboy* by Patricia Johns
*Texas Lullaby* by Tina Leonard
*The Texan's Little Secret* by Barbara White Daille
*The Texan's Surprise Son* by Cathy McDavid
*It Happened One Wedding Night* by Karen Rose Smith
*The Cowboy's Convenient Bride* by Donna Alward

## SHIPMENT 5

*The Baby and the Cowboy SEAL* by Laura Marie Altom
*The Bull Rider's Cowgirl* by April Arrington
*Having the Cowboy's Baby* by Judy Duarte
*The Reluctant Texas Rancher* by Cathy Gillen Thacker
*A Baby on the Ranch* by Marie Ferrarella
*When the Cowboy Said "I Do"* by Crystal Green

## SHIPMENT 6

*Aidan: Loyal Cowboy* by Cathy McDavid
*The Hard-to-Get Cowboy* by Crystal Green
*A Maverick to (Re)Marry* by Christine Rimmer
*The Maverick's Baby-in-Waiting* by Melissa Senate
*Unmasking the Maverick* by Teresa Southwick
*The Maverick's Christmas to Remember* by Christy Jeffries

## SHIPMENT 7

*The Maverick Fakes a Bride!* by Christine Rimmer
*The Maverick's Bride-to-Order* by Stella Bagwell
*The Maverick's Return* by Marie Ferrarella
*The Maverick's Snowbound Christmas* by Karen Rose Smith
*The Maverick & the Manhattanite* by Leanne Banks
*A Maverick under the Mistletoe* by Brenda Harlen
*The Maverick's Christmas Baby* by Victoria Pade

## SHIPMENT 8

*A Maverick and a Half* by Marie Ferrarella
*The More Mavericks, the Merrier!* by Brenda Harlen
*From Maverick to Daddy* by Teresa Southwick
*A Very Maverick Christmas* by Rachel Lee
*The Texan's Christmas* by Tanya Michaels
*The Cowboy SEAL's Christmas Baby* by Laura Marie Altom

# THE BULL
# RIDER'S COWGIRL

## April Arrington

Recycling programs
for this product may
not exist in your area.

ISBN-13: 978-1-335-52340-2

The Bull Rider's Cowgirl
First published in 2017. This edition published in 2022.
Copyright © 2017 by April Standard

This is a work of fiction. Names, characters, places and incidents are either the product of the author's imagination or are used fictitiously. Any resemblance to actual persons, living or dead, businesses, companies, events or locales is entirely coincidental.

For questions and comments about the quality of this book, please contact us at CustomerService@Harlequin.com.

Harlequin Enterprises ULC
22 Adelaide St. West, 41st Floor
Toronto, Ontario M5H 4E3, Canada
www.Harlequin.com

**Printed in U.S.A.**

**April Arrington** grew up in a small town and developed a love for books at an early age. Emotionally moving stories have always held a special place in her heart. April enjoys collecting pottery and soaking up the Georgia sun on her front porch.

Dedicated to my big brother, Steve.

I love you to the moon and back. Always.

## *Chapter 1*

*15.32. Left, right, right. Go for great.*

Only a fraction of a second separated a good barrel racer from a great one. The faster the run, the higher a name moved up the scoreboard. Tonight, Jen Taylor was determined her name would be at the top of the list.

"We can do this, Diamond."

Jen nudged her quarter horse into a jog across the grassy warm-up area. His white mane rippled over the edge of the saddle and fluttered against the reins. The crowd, inside Kissimmee's Silver Spurs Arena several feet away, burst into applause, signaling the end of another barrel racer's run.

"Easy." Jen dropped her weight in the saddle, took hold of the saddle horn and executed a sharp left turn.

She drew Diamond to a halt in front of the arena's alley entrance, sucked in a lungful of warm Florida air and tried to still the frantic flutters in her stomach. One more run and she'd be up. The clear April evening was a perfect night for racing. If she could just get a handle on her nerves…

"That was Autumn Langley of Texas," the announcer blared over the PA system.

Jen cringed, her face heating. Autumn Langley was one of the best in the arena. And a reminder of one of Jen's biggest humiliations outside it.

She craned her neck, focused on the illuminated board and tried to make out Autumn's score. The numbers and letters shifted. A few broke. Others floated. It was impossible to focus on them from this angle and her attention was too shot to concentrate.

Gut churning, she tore her eyes away. Diamond jerked his head and stomped his foot.

"It's okay, boy," she whispered, patting his neck.

Thankfully, the announcer spoke again.

"Give it up. Autumn just cranked out a 17.12…"

Jen released a slow breath. The time to beat was still 15.32.

Ignoring the tremble in her hands, Jen raked her gaze over the cluster of cowboys leaning on the fence inside the arena and focused on their relaxed expressions. In less than an hour, several of them would be battling to hang on to the back of a massive, bucking bull. But not a hint of anxiety showed on their faces.

"It's just another run," she said softly, weaving her fingers through Diamond's mane and drawing strength from the men's carefree features. "We're as strong on the dirt as any of those cowboys."

The man closest to the alley gate glanced up. His tan Stetson cast a shadow over his chiseled features and blond, close-cut beard beneath the floodlights. He straightened, his blue eyes finding her, and issued a tight smile.

Jen's belly warmed. Colt Mead's sexy grin and muscled form had always had that effect on her. As well as other parts of her anatomy. It never mattered where she was or what she was doing. All it took was one crooked grin from Colt and her blood rushed. Her mind shot straight to imagining what it would be like to be kissed by him. To have his strong hands running over her bod—

Her mouth twisted. It'd been that way since they'd first met, four years ago. Twenty years old, Jen had been touring the rodeo circuit alone for over a year. Colt, twenty-one at the time, rode bulls professionally. Jen had immediately pegged Colt for the player he was, but she'd still gotten a kick out of his flirtatious banter and it hadn't taken long for them to form a strong bond.

Only, there'd always been a sexual undercurrent to their friendship. One she'd been foolish enough to act on two weeks ago.

Colt leaned farther over the rail, his muscular bulk stretching his blue shirt and snug jeans. His smile vanished as he studied her expression.

Jen's breath caught at the hot effects of his sensual eyes traveling to her chest. An aggravating inconvenience, since he'd insisted they remain friends.

She dropped her gaze and squirmed. *Get it together, girl.*

Here she was, about to start a run, and her focus was on Colt. He was becoming a distraction. A threat to what she'd worked so hard to achieve. She had to perform well to get to the finals in Vegas. And she would. No matter how hard she had to work. That board at the Thomas & Mack arena was going to light up with her name at the top of the list.

There was no room in her life for a womanizer. Especially one who had already shot her down, then taken off with another woman. Autumn Langley, to be exact.

The gate clanged open. Autumn trotted out on her beige mare, her dark gaze narrowing on Jen's face.

Great. Just great. Of all the people to catch her salivating over Colt. And why the heck was Jen even concerned with either of them, anyway? She had a race to win.

Jen firmed her grip on Diamond's reins and looked away from them. Both of them... *together.* Her stomach roiled at the images flashing through her mind.

"Colt's looking fine these days." Autumn smirked and led her mare in a circle around Diamond. The rhinestones and elegant embroidery on her shirt glinted under the light spilling from the arena, drawing attention to her shapely figure. "Tell him to swing by my RV if he gets bored later." She laughed throatily. "That man knows how to give a woman a good time."

*Ignore her.* A bad run could make anyone angry. *Focus on winning.*

Jen lifted her chin and smiled. "I'll be sure to let him know."

"Good." Autumn's mouth flattened into a thin line, her voice curt. "He'll be grateful to you."

Jen dismissed the furious heat sparking through her veins and repositioned herself in the saddle. It wasn't any of her business who Colt spent time with. She knew he partied hard. Had watched firsthand as he'd sweet-talked women in the arena over the years. That was the very reason she'd initially refused to give in to her attraction to him.

One she should've remembered when she'd had too many beers, pulled a boneheaded move and kissed him. Instead, she'd suggested they act on their attraction, get it out of their system and consider being friends with benefits—behaving more like a buckle bunny than a seasoned, focused athlete.

She swallowed hard past the lump in her throat, finding it difficult to drag in air.

Autumn shook her head and tossed her black hair over her shoulder. "Dirt's bad in there." Her tone softened. "Makes for a tough run. Sure sucks being last."

*Last.* Jen winced. She'd always been last. The last student in her class to learn to read. A skill she'd struggled to master due to a learning disability. And the lowest ranked student in her graduating class. Her grades were the worst of all and far below the acceptable level of universities.

She hadn't let that stop her from pursuing success, though. No way was she going to end up just another small-town nothing. She'd gotten that high school diploma, found work on a local ranch and earned enough money to strike out on her own. Chasing a dream of making a name for herself in the one thing she'd always excelled at.

*Racing.* Jen flashed a brighter smile and met Autumn's stare head-on. "I don't mind bringing up the rear. Being last just makes you hungrier to be first."

That she knew from experience.

Autumn sighed, eyeing Diamond. "Seriously, girl. Take care out there. That roughed-up dirt can trip up any horse."

"Don't you have some cooling down to do, Autumn?" Tammy Jenkins, Colt's cousin and Jen's traveling partner, squeezed between the horses, her elbow bumping Jen's leg. "This is the warm-up ring."

"Warm-up ring?" Autumn scoffed, surveying the grassy patch surrounding them. "More like someone's backyard. No wonder everyone's time is off tonight, with no decent place to prepare."

"You're the only one whose time is off," Tammy said. "There's plenty of space to prepare and practice for those that put in the effort. You're just used to having things handed to you."

Jen's face heated. "Tammy—"

"No problem." Autumn held up a hand. "I know when I'm not wanted." She raised a brow and grinned. "Also know when I am. Don't forget to pass my message on to Colt." She tugged on her reins and walked her horse away, chiming over her shoulder, "It's always *so* nice talking to you, Tammy."

Tammy clucked her tongue. "That no good, trash-talking—"

"Calm down, Tammy." Jen stifled a laugh and reached down to squeeze her shoulder. "She was being decent for a change."

"Decent, my butt." Tammy crossed her arms, her green eyes flashing. "You cut people way too much slack. Autumn only speaks to you when she's up to something. She's trying to get in your head and trip you up. And no matter what she says, I don't believe Colt would ever be dumb enough to carouse with her."

Jen sighed. She could. Autumn wasn't just a talented racer. She was smart and attractive, too. And Colt had left the bar with her two weekends ago, his brawny arm around her waist and broad hand at her hip. Just a half hour after he'd slipped from Jen's drunken embrace on the bar stools.

"Doesn't matter." Jen ran shaky fingers through Diamond's mane. "Colt's fun to flirt with but I'm not interested in him in that way."

*"Right..."* Tammy's lips twitched. "I oughta kick you in the behind."

"For what?"

"For lying to your best friend. I've known for a while now that you have the hots for Colt. Anyone can see it on your face." Her lip curled in distaste as she glanced over her shoulder. "Even someone as self-absorbed as Autumn."

Jen's cheeks burned. Had it been that obvious?

"I'm just proud of you for staying focused and steering clear." Tammy gave a wry smile.

"And proud of him for respecting you enough to do the same. I love Colt, but he's trouble when it comes to women. He knows that." She frowned. "I don't know what's happened between the two of you lately, but I wish you'd straighten it out. It was bad enough listening to y'all flirt all the time, but it's worse with you not speaking to each other."

Jen's stomach flipped. If Tammy only knew what a fool she'd made of herself. And how much Colt's rejection had hurt...

No matter. She wasn't a schoolgirl anymore and knew the rules of the game. Colt was just another sexy bull rider on the circuit who wasn't looking for a relationship. Even a casual one. At least he'd been a good friend and had been honest with her up front.

"Hey." Tammy touched her arm. "The higher you are, the harder people try to pull you down. That's all Autumn was doing. Trying to pull you down." She patted Diamond's rump. "You and Diamond are the greatest pair tearing out of the alley. He hugs those barrels like they're his mama, and you rate him right on the money every time. Your skill surpassed mine and most other racers' a long time ago."

Jen doubted that. Other than Autumn,

Tammy was the best racer on the circuit. Tammy had taken Jen's breath away the night they'd met, blasting down the alley and breaking a barrel racing record. Several hours of practice together, thousands of laughs and a mutual love for the sport had led to a solid friendship.

A scattered round of groans sounded from inside the arena. The gate clanged open and a downbeat racer trudged out.

"Show the gal some love." The announcer's voice blared. "Knocking over barrels beats eating dirt, and she gave it her best. Time with penalties is 28.17, putting her in last position."

Jen renewed her grip on the reins, blood rushing and panic welling inside her again. She offered a sympathetic nod to the tearful brunette passing by on her mare.

"Where's your head, Jen?"

Jen glanced back down, her spirit lifting at Tammy's encouraging expression and gentle smile. There was no Autumn. No Colt. Just barrels and a run. Tammy was the best dang friend a girl could ask for.

"On tight," Jen said, tapping her hat down more firmly on her brow. "Can you remind me what the time to beat is?"

"15.32."

*Turn and burn.* Jen led Diamond to the alley. Rough dirt or not, that was exactly what she was gonna do.

Jen was still pissed. And he couldn't blame her.

Colt ducked his head and eased back from the fence as the most recent racer exited the arena. The speakers blared overhead on a stream of heavy metal as Jen made her way to the gate.

Colt tried to catch her eye again. Tried to get one more look at her face to reassure himself she'd shaken off the angry glare she'd shot him earlier and regained her focus. But her head was down, her hat making it impossible for him to get a clear view.

A fresh wave of tension assaulted his muscles. He uncurled his fists from the rail, flinching as his fingers cramped. Such a foolish state he'd worked himself into. He'd never gotten this tense over tangling with an angry bull. So why the hell would he get so terrified of watching a horse run around metal buckets?

"Arlene and I were together for seven weeks. *Seven damn weeks.* That's the longest I've stayed hooked up with any woman." His friend Judd Marsh, another bull rider, smacked the rail with his palm and vented at Colt's side. "She called it quits last night. Right after I got thrown off that nut job of a bull."

Colt winced. "Sorry, man."

"That ain't the worst of it, though. You know what she said to me?"

Colt shook his head.

"She said I don't pay her enough attention." He propped one hand on his hip, waved the other in the air and adopted a high-pitched voice. *"Judd, you're just not sensitive to my needs."* He slapped his leg and scowled. "Shit, man. I'm sensitive."

Colt bit back a laugh.

"Don't you think I'm sensitive?"

"Yep," Colt said. "Sensitive enough."

Colt's smile slipped. That was what he was becoming. What Jen was turning him into. Too damned sensitive. Which was exactly why he was standing here hyperventilating over the risk of Jen getting thrown off her horse despite the fact that she was a strong rider and it'd been months since her last fall.

Though it'd probably help if he didn't know how hard that dirt hurt when you slammed into it at high speed. Or how difficult it was to roll outta the way, get back on your feet and avoid a thousand-pound animal crushing the air out of your lungs.

Yeah. He might deal with it better if he hadn't experienced that himself.

"Hell. Whatever." Judd scanned the stands, gaze lingering over one section. "There's always another one out there."

Colt nodded. Judd was right on that count. There was always another woman. Plenty of them. And Colt had spent more nights than he cared to remember over the past four years trying to enjoy them. Only problem was, he no longer wanted them. Hadn't wanted anyone but Jen since the second he'd laid eyes on her.

He glanced to his left, managing to catch a quick glimpse of her face as she looked up before facing the barrels. Her long, red curls slipped over her shoulder, obscuring the curves of her cheek and mouth.

His body tightened. That mouth. That beautiful, soft mouth she'd used two weeks ago to whisper a sweet plea in his ear. That she'd trailed temptingly across the stubble on his cheek before kissing him.

What would those lush lips of hers have

felt like if he'd given in and kissed her back? Kissed her the way he'd wanted to for years? Deeply and passionately. How would she have responded? With slow, coaxing movements? Or hot, hungry—?

Colt jerked his head to the side. *Shut it down.* He had no right wondering. No right even contemplating it. Jen was too good a woman for a sexy, meaningless fling. And that'd never be enough for him, anyway. Not with her. Jen wasn't like the women he played with on the circuit. She was a competitive, focused athlete. One who wasn't impressed by smooth talk or skilled touches. She was above that. Deserved better.

A woman like Jen deserved a ring, a picket fence and a baby. The whole shebang. The kind of woman he wasn't interested in and wouldn't be any good with.

So he'd turned her down. He'd torn himself away before he had a chance to screw up and give in. Had arranged for a mutual friend he trusted to get her back to the motel safely, then had hauled ass with the first woman who threw herself in his path.

Colt's face tingled, his neck burning. He'd known just the sight of him leaving with another woman would tick Jen off enough to sober her up a bit and take her mind in another direction. She didn't need to know the farthest he'd gone with Autumn Langley was to the parking lot to help her into her truck. That he'd pulled a 180 right there on the cracked pavement and politely refused the rest of Autumn's advances.

He winced and rubbed his fingers over his cheek. Or that Autumn had smacked him a good one and accused him of leading her on. Using her to make Jen jealous. Which, no matter how good his intentions had been, was exactly what he'd done.

Yep. It was better he just be that guy. The one not worth crying over. That was the kind he'd been for years, anyway. The kind he'd always be.

"Next up, folks, is Jen Taylor." Cheers broke out around the arena at the announcement. "She hails from Hollow Rock, Georgia."

Colt straightened, hands grabbing the rail again.

Jen took her place at the top of the alley. She sat tall in the saddle, her red hair shining against her turquoise blouse, providing a fiery contrast to Diamond's white hide.

A shot of heat streaked through Colt. Damn, she was beautiful.

"Jen's partner is Diamond," the announcer shouted over the crowd, "though you probably know them as Fire and Ice."

The fans in the bleachers above Colt jumped to their feet, yelping as handfuls of their popcorn bounced off his hat. Colt's smile returned. Jen was good. Better than good. And everyone knew it. He'd seen her work her way up through grueling hours of practice, endless tours on the circuit and dogged determination.

The same determination that scared the hell out of him when she rode. She didn't hold back during a run. Wouldn't let Diamond, either. She burned across the dirt like a flame and Diamond curved around those barrels like a slick coating of frost.

"Jen looks ready," Judd said, nudging him with an elbow. "Think she can pull it off?"

"Hell, yeah."

*A 15.32?* Jen could crack that in her sleep. So long as she kept her focus.

Colt trained his gaze on Jen's face. Her brown eyes remained pinned to the pocket by the left barrel, lush lips moving slowly in a silent mantra. Diamond shuffled his feet in anticipation as he waited for her permission. A nod, a swift kick and they were off, blasting down the alley and heading for the first barrel at full speed.

The first turn was flawless. Jen checked him with two hands at just the right moment, gripped the saddle horn and led him around clean and easy. Diamond tore out of the turn and dashed to the next. The second rotation carried off without a hitch.

The pair blazed over to the last barrel but Diamond stumbled. His front hoof slipped on the uneven dirt, jerking Jen forward. The rail rattled under Colt's grip and his boot shot to the lower fence rung. His stomach heaved as the audience gasped.

"Hold on, Red," he bit out.

She did. Diamond regained his footing and darted around the last turn. Jen loosened the reins, giving Diamond control, and they blasted across the finish line to the applause of the crowd.

Colt relaxed and released his death grip on the fence.

"Damned shame," Judd said. "That trip's gonna cost her."

"Don't care." Colt pushed off the rail and headed for the exit. "She's still in one piece."

Though her pride had probably taken a hit at not earning the best time.

"Hey, where you going?" Judd called. "We're up soon."

"I know." Colt waved him off. "Be back in a minute."

With swift strides, he dodged whooping spectators under the blaring voice on the PA system.

"Beautiful ride by Jen Taylor. Time is 15.37, placing her second. Let's give that gal a hand..."

Nope. No way would Jen be happy with that. She'd said on more than one occasion that getting second only meant you were the first loser. Something he had a sudden desire to help her see differently.

Colt continued forcing his way through the chaotic mass of people. He'd made it several feet when a cry cut through the air at his side. A pink bundle banged into his left knee and he grabbed it before it tumbled to the floor.

A young girl—three, maybe four?—tossed her blond curls off her cute face and steadied herself with a small hand on his leg. She had brown eyes and freckles, just like his younger half sister, Meg. At least that was what he remembered. He'd last seen her when he left home seven years ago.

An uncomfortable ache formed in his gut.

One that appeared every time he remembered leaving Meg behind. "Whoa, there. You all right?"

The girl looked up at him, blinked, then spun back to scowl at the man chasing after her.

"But I want it!" Her outraged shriek almost took the roof off the arena.

"No, Annabelle." The man took her arm and tugged her back to his side. "You've already had one cotton candy and that's enough for tonight." He nodded at Colt, dragging a hand through his disheveled hair. "Sorry about that."

"No problem, man."

Colt glanced at the girl straining against her dad's hold. Her cheeks turned cherry red and her eyes squinted.

*Here it comes.* Colt did his best to navigate around the group in front of him and gain some distance.

"But Ty got two," she screeched. "I want two."

"Your brother only had one. The same as you. I said no and that's that."

She jerked away and hit the floor, her pink skirt flopping around her flailing legs. Her screaming sobs prompted everyone within a mile radius to frown in her dad's direction. He bent, hissed admonishments and tried to gather up her writhing form, with no success.

Colt cringed. Poor bastard. Kids might be cute but most of 'em turned out to be little devils disguised in pink ribbons or baseball caps. A man had to be crazy to saddle himself with one on a permanent basis.

The girl's cries strengthened, piercing Colt's ears and provoking a pained laugh from him. He shook his head and forged through the crowd, making his way outside. The fresh air enveloped him and the girl's shrieks faded.

"Hey." Tammy bumped him with her shoulder and fell in step beside him. Her lopsided smile didn't hold its usual sparkle. "Come to console our partner?"

Colt shrugged. "No need for consoling. Jen had a good run."

"Yeah. I know." Tammy nodded toward the outskirts of the warm-up area. "But try telling her that."

Jen was cooling Diamond down, apart from everyone at the edge of the grass. She walked him in slow lines, chin lifted. If Colt hadn't spent years studying every sweet curve of her body and how she moved it, he might've missed the overly stiff set of her shoulders and hard clench of her thighs around the saddle. But he didn't.

Colt cut his eyes away and watched the other racers mingling around the cooldown area. "I'm gonna touch base with her before I ride. You mind giving us a minute?"

"Sure." Tammy's brows raised, her green eyes encouraging as she walked away. "Take your time."

Colt walked over to Jen, stopping as she maneuvered Diamond into a turn and faced him. Her eyes flashed.

He squared his shoulders then nodded up at her. "That was a damn good run, Red."

Jen stilled and the hard glint in her eyes softened. She smiled. The action small and beautiful. But hesitant.

"Thanks." She patted Diamond's thick shoulder. "I've got a talented partner."

"It wasn't all him," Colt said. "You had a part in that, too. The hardest part." His hand lifted, reaching toward her. He brought it back to his side and shifted his stance. "Second place is fantastic considering the tough competition you had. You really were great."

Jen looked away, brushing light touches over Diamond's mane. Her smile fell. "Wasn't quite enough, though," she whispered.

Colt's throat closed. She was so hard on herself. More critical of her performances than anyone else was. Almost to the point of erasing all the joy from a competition. Her face had stopped lighting up at the start of a run like it used to. And at the moment he wanted to see that glow in her smile again. *Needed* to see it.

"It'll be more than enough next time," he said, freezing at the husky note in his voice.

Something soft heated his palm. He blinked and looked down, stiffening at the sight of his hand curled around her thigh, easing its way up toward her hip. Just as it had with so many other women.

Her rich, brown eyes narrowed their focus on his hand, then shot to his face. "Feeling sorry for me, Colt? Trying to help me feel better by throwing me a little attention?" Her face flushed and her voice shook. "I don't need soothing. But Autumn might. She said you're welcome to pay her a visit later." She eased Diamond back a few steps, sliding away from his touch. "Seems you're good at a lot more than just sweet-talking women."

Ah, hell. That was called for. But it stung. It squeezed his chest so tight, his lungs threatened to collapse.

Still, Jen's anger was an improvement over the defeated expression she'd had moments ago and a lot easier to deal with than her adoration. Especially since he knew that in the long run, he'd only disappoint.

"Yeah." He choked back his pride, knuckled his hat farther up his forehead and conjured a sly grin. "I am. You just haven't seen me at my best yet, baby." He widened his smile, easing back into the safe, familiar role. "Stick around and watch me ride."

Colt spun on his heel and ambled away. Jen's hard stare burned a bigger hole in his back with each step. He took the long way around to the bull pens, avoiding every buckle bunny and child within sight.

Women. He understood them only in the bedroom. And kids? He didn't understand them at all. Bulls, however, he got. And the massive, black-and-white-speckled monster glaring at him through the gate was about to get to know him, too.

## *Chapter 2*

"Careful. That son o' a bitch can spring."

Colt handed the end of his rope to Judd and studied the restless bull being prepared in the chute below them. "I hope so."

A bull that jumped, kicked and spun right out of the chute guaranteed a shot at a high score. The kind of score Judd had failed at grabbing several rides ago when he'd drawn a flat bull that took a Sunday stroll out of the chute instead of blasting out of it. Hopefully, Sonic, the burly beast Colt had drawn, would be feistier.

As if on cue, the angry animal slammed his thick horns into the metal rails, then sprang up, hooking his hooves over the top of the eight-feet-high gate. The cheers filling the Silver Spurs Arena strengthened as the cowboys surrounding the chute yanked on the ropes draped over the bull's back, pulling him off the gate.

Colt smiled. Hell, yeah. This one was a damn deal feistier.

He glanced around the arena, taking steady breaths and visualizing a successful scenario on the dirt. But his eyes snagged on a cream-colored hat and red hair in the stands.

In the front row, Jen no longer sat, but had shot to her feet, eyes on the bull banging around in the chute below him, and face creased with apprehension. Tammy and another woman he recognized as a barrel racer—Karla, was it?—stood at her side, looking equally dismayed.

Colt turned away, started wrapping tape around the glove on his left hand and did his best to ignore the warm satisfaction rippling through him. Pissed though she was, Jen had not only stuck around for over an hour to watch his ride, she was worried about him.

"Told you this joker could spring," Judd shouted over the hard rock music. "You ready to get slung?"

"Yep." Colt bit the tape off, handed the roll to one of the spotters at his side and jerked his chin. "So long as it's after eight seconds."

A buzzing in Colt's back pocket rattled through the denim of his jeans. He yanked his cell phone out, glancing at the lit screen. Mead Enterprises.

Colt shook his head. Friday night. Approaching 10:00 p.m. No doubt his father, John W. Mead, would still be holed up in his high-rise Atlanta office closing another deal. It was always about business with John W. Mead. Never personal. And never about actually building a relationship with his son. That had become especially true after Colt's mother died.

Nope. His old man probably wanted the same thing he'd been hassling him about for the last year.

*Time to get your ass home, Colt. You've played long enough and there's work to be done.*

Colt rejected the call with a rough swipe of his thumb and shoved his cell toward Judd. "Mind hanging on to that till I'm through?"

"Sure." Judd shoved it in his pocket, then firmed his grip on the rope.

Colt scrutinized Sonic's movements and

regained his focus. He shoved in his mouth guard, grabbed the opposite rail and climbed into the chute, placing a boot in the center of the bull's back. He waited a couple seconds as Sonic shifted and stomped, then slid his legs down around the bull's muscular sides and sat.

The rich scent of musky hide filled his nostrils and the tang of dirt drifting on the air touched his tongue with each breath he took. He grabbed hold of the rope Judd stretched up, and yanked his gloved hand over it briskly, tapping it with his fist when he finished to cue Judd to hand it over. Hooking his gloved fingers through the handle laying over the bull's back, he set the rope, then wrapped the long end of it around his palm. He closed his fist, opened it, then curled it again.

Satisfied with his grip, Colt secured his position, then nodded.

The gate clanged open and Sonic catapulted into the arena, his back end twisting and lifting vertically several feet into the air on a vicious kick. Colt stretched his right arm high above his head as they rose up. He leaned back and the muscles in his left forearm seized with his strained grip on the rope.

Sonic's hard haunches slammed against

Colt's shoulder blades. The bull's long tail whipped over Colt's head and smacked across his face, the coarse hairs stinging his eyes and knocking his hat off his head.

Gravity snatched them back down and Sonic's front hooves hit the dirt, yanking Colt forward. Colt jerked his head to the side, his cheek missing the sharp point of a horn by inches.

Sonic lurched again, lifting them both so high so fast that Colt's gut swirled on an intense wave of panicked excitement. A shout exploded from deep within his chest and blasted through the smile stretching across his mouth guard.

*Hot damn!* This beast could fly.

Clenching his thighs to counteract each of Sonic's moves, Colt held on with his left fist, but let go of the world around him. The spectators' cheers dimmed to barely discernable echoes and the violent thrashings of the bull rattled away every care or concern he'd ever had.

They soared, spun, then thudded hard against the earth. Over and over. Each of their grunts and harsh breaths flooded Colt's senses as he pitted his will against Sonic's.

A buzzer sounded and reality struck, ripping his attention away from the battle and back to survival. He wrestled his hand free of the rope and leaned to the side as Sonic writhed in the air, allowing the momentum to sling him from the bull's back and tumble him across the dirt.

He sprang to his feet and ran. Sonic followed, charging twice before the bullfighters distracted him and directed him back toward the pen.

Colt spotted his Stetson in the dirt. He scooped it up, settled it back on his head, then tipped the brim at Sonic. The bull snorted, kicking the metal gate one more time as he bulldozed his way into the pen.

Colt pulled his mouth guard out, shoved it in his pocket and laughed. "Nice meetin' you, too, you big bastard."

He waved at the cheering crowd, then made his way out of the ring, rubbing a hand over the sore muscles of his lower back and grimacing at the sharp ache in his left ankle.

Judd met him at the gate, handed him his phone, then slapped his shoulder. "I think you just locked this one down, man. No one's going to pull off a better ride than that tonight."

"Let's hope not," Colt said, breathing hard. "That bull made me earn it."

Judd laughed. "I gotta get back and spot another rider." He jerked his thumb over his shoulder as he left. "Your fan club's calling."

Colt glanced toward the stands. Tammy stood on the floor beside the front row, laughing and waving her hat wildly. Karla was at her side, whistling through two fingers and making catcalls. Jen stood nearby with a blank expression, clutching a beer.

Colt made his way over but slowed when Jen's dark eyes ran over him, hovering on the slight limp of his left leg. His grin widened and that tingle of satisfaction returned.

"That was fantastic," Karla yelled over the noise in the arena.

"Fantastic?" Tammy threw her arms around his shoulders and squeezed. "It was phenomenal!"

A chuckle escaped him despite the painful twinge Tammy's snug hold caused. "Glad you thought so."

"Are you all right?"

Jen scrutinized his left leg. Her eyes lifted and locked with his, the gentle concern shining there sparking an unwelcome yearning in his chest. It made his palms itch with the need to reach out and tug her to him. Made him miss the friendly banter they used to share.

"Why?" Colt slipped out of Tammy's embrace and flashed a cocky grin, teasing her like he used to. "Worried about me, baby?"

Jen didn't respond in kind as he'd hoped. Just scoffed, her mouth flattening as she cut her eyes away.

He wasn't sure what got under her skin more. The suggestive tone he'd used or the arrogant smile he'd adopted. Though it could've been the wink he'd thrown in, too.

What he did know for sure was that the damage he'd done that night in the bar caused all three actions to fall flat and made him feel like more of a heel than ever.

Tammy's small fist punched his chest. "Watch it, Colt."

Duly chastised, he ducked his head and ignored the heat singeing his cheeks.

"After you collect your check, we need to pack up and head out," Tammy said. "That big money pot is still up for grabs at the Davie Pro Rodeo tomorrow night and I could use the extra time to prepare. I really need that win if I'm going to make it to the finals this year."

"You've got nothing to worry about," Colt said, squeezing her shoulder.

Tammy's brows rose. "Oh yeah, I do. You

think Jen felt bad about placing second to-night? I'd have killed for that spot. I was fifth, Colt. *Fifth*."

"I know, but—"

"And I was eighth," Karla added, tucking a short strand of black hair behind her ear. "Tammy and I have already crunched some numbers. Jen can get by without another win this weekend, but if Tammy and I don't place in the top three at Davie, we'll be so far be-hind we'll never qualify for Vegas."

"You'll make it," Colt said, meeting Tam-my's uncertain expression with a determined one. "I know you will."

"Not if I don't place at Davie tomorrow night." Tammy shook her head. "Without that win, I'm out."

Colt nodded. A trip to Davie was just in time. Maybe he'd have more luck finding a woman there who stirred his interest. One who would help him shake off this lust he had for Jen. Then maybe he'd have a decent shot at rebuilding their friendship.

"So we'll head to Davie." He grinned and patted his front pocket. "Right after I collect my check."

Yep. That was the way he liked it. No bag-gage. No responsibilities. Just an endless string of nights filled with fun and freedom. All provided by the bulk of bills lining his pockets. Money he'd earned himself on the back of a bull. Free and clear of his corporate raider father.

The phone in Colt's hand went off, jerking with rhythmic pulses. He glanced at the screen. Mead Enterprises again.

He groaned. John W. Mead wasn't giving up tonight. Might as well get it over with.

"Gotta take this." Colt nodded in apology to the ladies, exited the arena and accepted the call, striving for a nonchalant tone. "Before you ask, I'm headed south. In the opposite direction."

Silence hung heavy on the line. There was no sharp reprimand from his father. No cynical comeback. Just empty air.

Colt huffed out a breath and kicked the ground. The old man was trying a new tactic. "Go ahead. Lay that guilt on thick 'cause it doesn't matter. I'm not interested in joining up with the company. I have business of my own to take care of." Bulls. Beaches. And beauties. Not necessarily in that order. "You hear me, Dad?"

"Mr. Mead? Colt Wyatt Mead?"

He stilled. The voice on the other end of the line was feminine. Hesitant but businesslike.

"You got him. Who's this?"

"This is Angela Reed. Your father's secretary."

Colt's fingers squeezed the phone, his laugh hesitant. "You're working late tonight. He ask you to pass along new marching orders to me?"

"Sir." A swift intake of air sounded across the line. "I'm sorry to deliver news this way but…" An odd tapping started, as if a phone cord was being jiggled. "There was—" Her voice cracked. "Your father's partner, Jack Evans, has been trying to reach you. He asked me to call and tell you…"

He froze. "Tell me what?"

"There's been an accident." Her words were short and swift. "Your father's jet crashed this morning. I'm sorry to say he didn't make it."

Colt's stomach heaved, a wave of nausea surging over him. "What?"

"I'm very sorry, Mr. Mead," she whispered. "But Mr. Evans wanted you to know in time to return home for the funerals if you desired to do so. Services have been arranged for Sunday afternoon."

*"Funerals?"* Dear God. *Meg.* "My sister. Was she—"

"No, sir," she said hastily. "Your sister wasn't on board. Just your father and Mrs. Mead."

A strange tingling spread over him, buzzing through his blood and clouding his vision. The ground warped beneath his feet. He moved closer to the paddock fence in front of him and grabbed at the top rail.

His father. His stepmother. *Dead.*

"Mr. Mead?" The secretary's voice softened. "Your sister is the other reason for my call. There are several matters that require your attention. May I tell Mr. Evans that you'll be returning?"

Colt squeezed his eyes shut. His throat thickened, strangling his words. "Y-yes. I'm returning."

The trembling in his limbs turned violent. Colt cut the call and clenched both hands into fists. He continued standing there as winners were announced over the PA system. Stayed still as the throng of spectators left the arena and made their way to the parking lot, leaving only rodeo participants behind.

Colt waited until his stomach hardened and the feeling in his limbs vanished. Until there was no feeling left anywhere. Numb was a damned sight better than breaking down right now. He had to stay in control to make the long drive home. And he was a world away from Atlanta's Tuxedo Park.

"Colt?"

Jen took a few hesitant steps forward, her boots whispering over the grass as she approached him. He didn't answer. Just stood there, motionless as he stared straight ahead at the paddock, fists at his sides.

The crowd outside the Silver Spurs Arena had dwindled to a few rodeo riders, every one of them eager to find the next party and unwind. All except Colt. One phone call had extinguished his flirtatious demeanor.

Jen's skin prickled at the unusually tight set of his broad shoulders. She stopped, fiddled with the soggy label on her beer and tried again.

"Colt. What's wrong?"

A crack of laughter rang out. Jen glanced over her shoulder to find Tammy and Karla sauntering through the exit and sharing a joke.

Tammy's eyes brightened as they landed on Colt. "Well, finally. We've been waiting for you for forever. You won. They've got your check…"

Her steps faltered at his lack of response and she shot a look at Jen.

Jen shook her head.

"Who was on the phone, Colt?" Tammy moved to his side and placed a hand on the small of his back, releasing a small laugh. "Come on. You're scaring us. Who was it?"

A muscle in his jaw ticked. "My father's secretary."

"Bad news?" Tammy asked.

He nodded.

"Well, wha—"

"My father's dead."

Tammy gasped and wrapped her hand around his upper arm. "Oh, no."

Jen froze, her fingers clutching the beer bottle hard. Karla made a sound of dismay at her side.

"He and my stepmom." His brow furrowed. "Their jet crashed."

The words were flat. Emotionless. His blue eyes were empty and his expression remained stoic.

Jen's vision blurred. "I'm so sorry, Colt," she whispered, unsure what else to say.

They rarely spoke of family. His, Tammy's or hers. Just made vague comments when necessary. He and Tammy were close and that was about as much as she knew.

Colt's features hardened and he shrugged away from Tammy's touch. "They always flew on a private jet." A muscle ticked in his jaw. "It's faster and my father says it's safer. At least that's what he used to say." A sneer crossed his face. "Truth was, he thought he was too good to fly commercial with common people. Both of them did." His voice weakened. "Death doesn't discriminate, though, does it?"

Jen's heart squeezed at the shadows in his eyes. She glanced at Tammy, her throat closing at the tears streaming down her friend's cheeks. Jen crossed to her side and squeezed her hand.

Colt planted his back to them, saying, "My sister's alone."

"You have a sister?" Jen asked.

Colt nodded and thrust his hands in his pockets. "Meg. My half sister. She's around nine now. I haven't seen her since she was two."

Jen hesitated. "Surely a family member's with her—"

"What family?" Scorn tinged his words. He spun around to face her. "My father's work was his family. It's not surprising that his secretary was the one to give me the news." He hesitated, his sculpted mouth opening, then closing as he eyed his cousin. "Tammy, I need to go home. Just for the weekend. For the funeral and to see Meg."

"Of course." Tammy pulled her hand free from Jen's and wiped her cheeks. "I'll go with you. We can have the horses loaded in no time."

"No." Colt held up a hand. "I'm going alone. You have a race to win."

Tammy's jaw fell. "Screw the race, Colt. I'm not—"

"You *are*." He shook his head, jaw clenching. "You know what it's like back there. And I'm not staying for any longer than the..." He stopped, looking away before continuing. "I'm not staying any longer than necessary."

Jen ached at the bleak tone in his voice. She longed to wrap her arms around Colt and comfort him but knew he wouldn't accept it.

"Colt." Tammy's tone turned hard. "There's no way I'm letting you go alo—"

"You don't have to let me do anything. This is how I want it." Colt's chest lifted on a rough breath. "You knew what he was like. He never gave a shit about me. Or you. Or anyone for that matter. I'm not letting you blow your chance at success for that—"

His voice cracked. He spun on his heel to leave.

Tammy grabbed his arm and jerked him to a stop. "Colt. This is ridiculous." She stepped close, her face pleading. "You can't expect me to waltz off to a race while you're dealing with this."

"You think I'd want you going back there? Ever?" Colt took her shoulders and peered down at her. "Do you *want* to go back, Tammy?"

Jen studied her friend. Tammy looked down, hands twisting and face paling.

Colt's chin trembled. He dragged his teeth over his bottom lip. "You weren't welcome there before he died. You think you'll be more welcome now? Take my word for it that whoever he left in charge of that place will be just as cold and hateful as he was. I'm not letting you go through that again."

"Colt, please. You can't..." A sob broke from Tammy.

Colt tugged her close and tucked her head under his chin, his voice strained. "You'll go to Davie and you'll win. And I'll be back before you know it."

Jen closed her eyes, her heart still clenching at the mixture of pain and tenderness in Colt's face.

"Then let Jen go with you."

Jen's eyes sprang open at Tammy's words. "What? Tammy—"

Tammy spun to face her, expression fierce. "I can't let him go alone, Jen. And you'll be fine without competing at Davie."

"No," Colt stated, stepping back.

Tammy followed and grabbed Colt's vest. "Let her go with you. If for no other reason than to make sure you get there and back safely. There's no way I'll be able to focus tomorrow night knowing you're dealing with this on your own." She jerked her chin at Karla. "You traveling to Davie alone?"

Karla nodded.

"You mind me and Razz catching a ride with you? That way Jen can take Diamond with Colt. I'll pitch in for gas and expenses."

"Of course," Karla said. "I'd be happy to help."

Jen shook her head. "Tammy, this is not a good idea."

"Jen's right. I'll be fine on my own." Colt pulled free of Tammy and walked back into the arena.

Tammy hesitated, staring after Colt for a

moment. Then she rushed to Jen, taking her forearms, hard and desperate. "You've got to do this for me, Jen. I'll talk to him. He'll be fine with it."

"I know you're worried," she said gently. "But you heard him. He wants to go alone."

"Colt wants to do a lot of things that aren't good for him. And he usually does." Tammy's small smile died quickly. "But this is one time that I can't let him. Please, Jen. I know him. He needs someone right now no matter what he says. Too much has happened for him to let me go back—" She bit her lip and waved a hand in the air. "There's no way he'll bend on letting me go, but he will for you." She stepped forward, hugged Jen and whispered, "No matter what went down between you two, I know you care about him as much as I do. Colt and I are lucky we found you. You're not just a friend to us. You've become family. I know you'll take care of Colt and I know he needs you. It's only for the weekend. So, please, do this for me."

Something wet tickled Jen's cheek. She rubbed it off on Tammy's shoulder and huffed out a breath.

Tammy laughed and released her, brushing a new flood of tears from her face, too.

"I may love you like a sister but that doesn't mean you can use my shirt as a hanky."

"That's what you get for being so sappy." Jen smiled, blinking hard to clear her vision. "I'll go. But only if he agrees to it."

"He will." Tammy headed after Colt, calling over her shoulder, "I'll be back in a few minutes to help load up, Karla."

Jen watched Tammy leave and felt the weight of Karla's stare, her cheeks heating under her scrutiny. Jen glanced away and stood still as fellow racers laughed and climbed into their vehicles. Engines turned over and trucks began lining up on the paved road leading to the exit. No doubt once the night's fun was had, they'd rise early tomorrow morning, hook up their trailers and head to the next event. Davie, most likely.

Jen looked down at the soggy beer label and picked at the corners. If she went with Colt, she'd miss the Davie Pro Rodeo. Lose an opportunity to gain a better advantage over her competitors. And she'd have to work that much harder to earn a ticket to Vegas when she returned.

Only, seeing Colt in pain had tied a knot in her chest that she didn't think would disappear when she hit the alley at Davie.

"Tammy's right." Karla dragged the toe of her boot over the grass and shoved her hands in her pockets. "I've never seen Colt clam up like that before. It's good you're going with him."

"Yeah," Jen whispered. "It's a good thing."

She hoped it was. A couple days. That was all. She'd help Colt through this, then she'd plan a new schedule, get back on the road and hit the circuit again.

Aside from their recent falling out, Colt had always been a good friend to her. It was time for her to be a good friend to him. Just as long as she remembered being friends was all he wanted. And all she could afford to be.

## Chapter 3

Colt rubbed a hand over his gritty eyes and sat up straight in the driver's seat. The entrance was close, about three blocks ahead. He'd know it as soon as he saw it. There'd be a broad metal gate, security checkpoint and endless paved driveway.

He glanced in the rearview mirror, cocking his head and straining for any abnormal sounds from the white trailer hitched to his truck. Diamond was quiet. Just as he had been the entire eight-hour drive from Kissimmee to Atlanta. It seemed he'd taken full advantage of the quiet night drive to sleep and wasn't ready to start his Saturday morning yet.

"Where are we?"

Jen pushed up from her slumped position in the passenger's seat, blinking slowly. The soft glow of the dashboard instruments was the only light in the dark stillness of the truck's cab.

Colt managed a small smile before looking away. Jen had been quiet, too. She'd stopped her gentle attempts at conversation and gone to sleep six hours ago, after he'd refused her offer to drive. Desperate for a distraction, he'd held on to his position behind the wheel, focusing on the road instead of the burning ache in his throat.

He'd fought against Jen coming. Had argued with Tammy for a good ten minutes and made it clear that he preferred to make the trip alone. The fear of breaking down in front of Jen was as unsettling as the challenge he already faced. But Tammy had refused to budge, and he had to admit that traveling the dark stretch of the interstate had been less grueling with someone at his side.

Even if that someone had every right to be angry with him and every reason not to offer her support.

"Colt?" Jen thumbed her hat higher on her

forehead, her brown eyes searching his face. "Where are we?"

His smile fell. "Tuxedo Park."

Colt looked out the window at the streetlights underscoring the lush greenery lining the road. The urge to hit the brakes, swing the truck in the opposite direction and drive for days was strong. He wanted nothing more than to forget. To pretend last night hadn't happened and return to the status quo. Imagine that he'd never gotten the call and learned—

He clutched the steering wheel tighter. That was one thing he couldn't do. No amount of distractions could change the fact that his father and stepmother were gone. Or that Meg was now the only remaining member of his immediate family.

The entrance appeared. Tall trees and shrubs lined each side of it.

Colt slowed the truck, maneuvered the sharp turn and stopped at the gate. A guard leaned out of the security office's entrance and waited for Colt to let down the window.

"Good morning, sir." He swept a flashlight briefly through the interior of the cab, then over the trailer. "May I ask who you're visiting?"

Colt didn't recognize him. Not that he would recognize any of the staff after a seven-year absence. His father had consumed them like water, always finding fault with even the best employees and promptly trading them out for new ones.

Colt leaned to the side and dug in his back pocket for his wallet. "Meg Mead."

"Is she expecting you?"

He winced. "Probably not."

"May I see your identifi—" The guard stopped as Colt pressed his ID into his hand, then flicked his flashlight over it. "Thank you, Mr...." He glanced up, eyes widening. "Mr. Mead?"

"Yeah."

"I'm sorry for your loss, sir."

Colt nodded.

"I apologize, Mr. Mead, but..." The guard motioned toward the inside of the cab. "I'll need to see—"

"Of course." Colt glanced at Jen. "He needs your license, Red."

Her brows raised but she murmured an assent, bending over to the floorboard and fishing her ID out of her purse. Colt took it and handed it over, watching as the man examined it, then flashed his light into the cab.

"Could you remove the hat, please, miss?"

Colt's jaw tightened. *Procedures.* His father had insisted on them being followed to the letter. So much so that his expectations were still met despite the fact that he was as good as in the ground.

Jen removed the leather cowgirl hat, tucking it between her knees and brushing her red bangs back. The guard tipped the flashlight up, flooding Jen's face. She squinted and shrank back against the door.

Colt hissed in a breath and threw up a hand to block the glare. "It's fine. Open the gate."

"Yes, sir."

The guard handed him the license, stepped back and buzzed the gates open, which swung out in wide arcs. Colt shifted gears, accelerating through them and heading down the winding, paved path ahead. They drove in silence for a few minutes, the headlights illuminating clusters of trees and healthy plants with bright, bountiful blooms on either side of the wide driveway.

Jen tossed her hat in the back of the extended cab and rubbed her palms over her jean-clad thighs. "Pretty intense security for a subdivision."

"This isn't a subdivision." Colt pressed

his foot harder on the pedal, plowing up the steep incline in front of them. "It's my father's house."

She laughed, the sound short and nervous as she took in the thick foliage surrounding them. "There's a house? Where?"

When they cleared the top of the hill, the sun broke over the surrounding trees, flooding the sprawling grounds with light.

Colt tipped his head toward the massive structure in front of them. "There."

Jen stilled, lips parting. He followed her gaze and gritted his teeth as he surveyed the familiar estate. A French provincial–style mansion consisting of thirty-five thousand square feet of space, stables, theater, pool, tennis court and caretaker's suite sat center stage on a manicured twenty-acre lot.

"That's not a house," she whispered.

Colt sighed. "I know."

He guided the truck around the circular drive, rounded a large churning fountain and brought them to a halt. After cutting the engine, he glanced up to find Jen studying him.

Her eyes narrowed, scrutinizing his features as though she didn't recognize him. She turned her back to him and stared up at the massive flight of stairs that led to the double door entrance. "I wish Tammy were here."

Her words were so soft he barely caught them. But he did.

He squeezed his eyes shut, wishing circumstances were different and that Tammy could be here, too. She kept him grounded. Reminded him of who he really was and, most importantly, who he didn't want to become.

His gut roiled. The kind of person his father had been. The kind of person Jen had just searched for when she'd inspected his face. A pompous, entitled man who put his own desires above the needs of others.

"Why wouldn't you let her come?" Jen asked, turning to him. "I mean, besides the race. I know that can't be your only reason."

Colt looked away and placed his hands on the steering wheel. "Tammy's mom was my dad's sister. My dad had basically disowned her. She'd blown all her money, lived hard and apparently wasn't worth knowing anymore. Tammy's dad and mine were both cruel. But where my dad just used his words, Tammy's liked to use his fists. And her mom did nothing to stop it."

The air grew thick and heavy in the cab. His throat closed and he swallowed, waiting for Jen to speak. When she didn't, he forced himself to continue.

"Things got so bad, Tammy finally called me and asked for help. I was seventeen. A dumb kid, thinking if I brought Tammy here, my dad might actually man up and do something." Colt tightened his grip on the wheel, his nails cutting into his palms. "Suffice it to say, he made it clear Tammy didn't belong here. And I already knew I didn't, either. So when I turned eighteen, I left and took Tammy with me."

"How did you end up on the circuit?"

Hearing Jen's shaky voice, Colt glanced over. The tear slipping from her dark lashes sent a stabbing pain through his chest.

"Riding bulls was a quick way to make money and I found out I was pretty good at it. Tammy knew horses and I made enough to set her up to race." A bitter laugh burst from his lips. "We were both angry at the world in general. Riding bulls let me fight back and racing horses let Tammy run. Tammy wasn't born tough. She was made that way. And there's no way in hell I'd ever let her revisit what got her there."

A soft sound escaped Jen. She leaned over and wrapped him in a hug.

A wave of soothing heat swept over him,

causing his hands to dig into the silky fall of her hair and his body to hum. He longed to tug her closer, drive away and leave it all behind. But Meg needed him and his focus should be on her. Not Jen.

Colt held on for a few moments, then forced himself to let go, pull away and jerk his chin toward the main house.

"I might as well get this over with."

Jen ducked her head, her cheeks flooding with color. She grabbed her purse and whispered, "I need to take care of Diamond before we go in."

He nodded and opened his door, forcing himself to ignore the sudden desire to ease back into her comforting hold and explore her inviting mouth.

It took a few minutes to unload Diamond. By the time they'd managed it, a groundskeeper approached, offering assistance, and Jen reluctantly handed Diamond's care over to a stable hand. Colt retrieved their overnight bags and they made their way up the steep flight of stairs to the front entrance, pausing two-thirds of the way to catch their breath.

"This is ridiculous," Jen muttered, glancing below them at the truck.

Colt relieved her of her bag. "*Too* ridiculous."

Her eyes locked with his and they both laughed, his rigid muscles relaxing and his pain easing. Thank God she was here.

A click sounded as a door swung open. Jen's laughter died on her lips. Colt's chuckle trailed away, too, and he turned to find a tall, slim woman standing in the open doorway. She stood motionless in a stiff-collared shirt and dark slacks, her only greeting a stern expression.

"Hey," Colt called, shielding his eyes from the glare of the sun. "I'm here to see Meg Mead."

"It's a bit early for visitors," the woman replied, tucking a stray gray hair back into her updo. "I'm Ms. Parks, Margaret's nanny. May I have your name, please?"

Colt bit back a retort. His father's strict protocols were always followed and it was routine for guests to be announced once they passed the outer gates. She'd known who he was long before his boots ever hit the driveway.

Forcing a polite smile, he climbed the last few stairs to the front door. "I'm Colt Mea—"

He jerked to a halt when they reached the landing.

The sharp glare of the sun's rays shifted and he could just make out a young girl's face peeking around the woman's hip. Blond hair, brown eyes.

Colt's chest burned. "Meg?" His voice emerged in a rasp and he set the bags down, clearing his throat.

"Margaret, I asked you to wait inside." The woman reached behind her and tapped the child's shoulder. "Since you're here, you may as well come out and introduce yourself properly."

The girl blinked, her guarded eyes moving from Colt to Jen and back, but made no move to step forward.

Colt dragged his clammy palms over his thighs. "Do you know who I am, Meg?"

She stepped around the woman and straightened, the top of her head barely reaching his waist. "No one calls me that."

He let out a slow breath, his smile tentative. "I used to."

Her small mouth tightened. "I don't remember."

Colt's gut churned. Her frown was overly fierce and the tilt of her chin too pronounced. She kept cutting looks at Jen, brows drawing farther down.

"That's okay," he said gently. "I remember. I'm Colt. Your brother."

His tongue clung to the roof of his mouth, the last word foreign and strange.

The woman at Meg's side twisted her hands together and her nose wrinkled slightly.

"My name is Margaret." Her fingers picked at the hem of her khaki skirt, which brushed the tops of her knees. "That's what everyone calls me."

Colt examined her as she shifted from foot to foot. Her shoes were a shocking hot pink, but she had on navy blue knee-highs and a matching collared shirt with an emblem.

His throat ached. "Are you on the way to school, Margaret?"

"No. I just got back. The driver doesn't pick me up for weekends until six on Saturday mornings. I stay Friday night to take music lessons. We pay extra for private ones. Mr. Evans told me yesterday on the phone that Dad always said..." Her chin wobbled. "Mr. Evans said you can never get too far ahead. And that I shouldn't miss a lesson, no matter what."

*Mr. Evans.* Colt scoffed. Jack Evans. His father's business partner.

Jen shifted at his side and touched her fingertips to her lips, features strained. Ms. Parks's face flushed and she smoothed a hand over Meg's blond curls.

A spark of anger lit in Colt's gut. Ten years older than Colt, Jack had been a hanger-on from the moment he'd entered their lives, clawing his way into the family business and endearing himself as a second son. Enough so that he'd taken it upon himself to deliver the devastating news to Margaret. By phone, no less. Then hadn't even bothered to bring her home early.

Colt shook his head. "Margar—"

"Who's she?" Margaret stared at Jen, eyes flashing over her from head to toe.

"This is Jen Taylor. A friend of mine."

Jen smiled, bent and offered her hand. "Hi, Margaret."

"Hello." Margaret kept her arms at her sides, looking down at her pink shoes for a moment before glancing back up. She surveyed Jen's outstretched hand, then the other one, and squinted up at her. "What should I call you? Miss Taylor? Or Miss Jen?"

Jen shrugged, hand and smile dropping. "Whatever you want. Jen is fine."

"Was that your horse they took to the stables?"

"Yes. His name's Diamond." Jen slipped her hands in her back pockets, her tone nervous. "You saw us pull up?"

Margaret nodded. "They always announce guests. I watched from the window." She examined Jen again, her brown eyes narrowing on Jen's jeans and clinging to the shiny rhinestones ringing the front pockets. "Those are some tight pants."

"Margaret," Ms. Parks admonished. "Your manners."

Colt tensed. *Nice effort.* But the nanny's disapproving glance at Jen proved she agreed with Margaret's declaration.

"I'm sorry," Margaret muttered. "But they *are* some tight pants."

Jen's mouth twitched and she gestured to Margaret's feet, smile returning. "Those are some bright shoes." She winked, adding softly, "I like them. A lot."

Margaret nibbled on her bottom lip, digging the toe of her right sneaker into the doormat and dodging Jen's gaze.

Colt lowered himself to his knees and nudged her chin up with a knuckle. "I'm sorry, Margaret."

"For what?" she mumbled, still looking down.

He grimaced. "For Dad and Rach—"

"Why?" Her eyes shot to his face, narrowing to slits. "She wasn't your mother. She was mine."

His breath caught at the reminder. Rachel had been his third stepmother. And hadn't cared for him any more than the other two. "I know."

"She was *mine*," she repeated, rosebud mouth trembling.

Her lashes spilled over and a large tear slipped down each cheek, dripping off her chin and plopping onto her shirt. Colt's body felt heavy. But he lifted his arms, drawing Margaret close and enfolding her in a loose embrace.

"I'm sorry," he whispered, leaning down and brushing a kiss across her cheek.

She jumped and shoved him back, scrubbing her hands across her face. "That hurts."

Colt held up shaky hands. "What?"

*"That."* She jabbed a finger at his chin.

He blinked and touched his jaw, the stubble of his beard rough against his fingertips.

"You came for the house, didn't you? That's why you're here." Margaret jerked her chin at Jen. "That's why she's here. Mr. Evans said Dad left it to us and that you'd come for it."

Margaret had composed herself again. There were no more tears. No chin wobble.

Just a defiant, judgmental expression. So like their father's. The pain in Colt's chest flooded his veins, coursing in hot streaks through his body.

"Where is Jack, Ms. Parks?"

"Mr. Mead," the nanny said, stepping between them. "Perhaps it's best if—"

"*Where*—" Colt gritted his teeth "—is he?"

"In Dad's study." Margaret nodded. "He said you'd come."

"Wait here, Red." Colt stood and eased around Margaret, taking long strides across the foyer.

"Colt?" Jen's voice shook.

He paused, glancing over his shoulder. A worried shadow lurked in Jen's eyes as they swept over his frame.

"I'll just be a minute." He softened his tone. "Promise."

She didn't look convinced. Colt spun and made his way down the long corridor, finding the marble floor and walls as cold and hard as he remembered them. He gripped the thick handles of the wide double doors leading to his father's study and shoved them open.

Jack Evans sat behind a massive, ornate desk. His dark head was bent over a pile of scattered files and folders, and the shiny pen he held flashed under the lamplight with each movement of his hand.

"Making yourself at home?"

Jack stilled. He clicked the pen, placed it on the desk and rose. "Colt."

He looked the same. Lean. Polished. Professional. And as bland as the slate-gray suit and tie he wore.

"It's good to see you," Jack said, sliding his hands in his pockets and rocking back on his heels. "Though I wish it were under different circumstances."

Slick bastard. Words were the cheapest thing in this high-priced mansion.

Jack hesitated at the silence, dipping his head and saying, "It's a difficult time for all of us."

"Yeah." Colt sneered. "I can see you're all torn up about it."

Jack jerked his hands from his pockets. "Really? This is where we're going to start?" He straightened his tie, tucking it beneath the edge of his jacket. "Picking right back up where you left off, aren't you?"

"What? By being honest? That's the only way I operate." A hard smile stretched Colt's cheeks. "I'm sure the concept's alien to you."

"Cut the shit, Colt." Jack shook his head.

"You haven't come by anything honestly. Don't have a clue what it's like to work to the bone for something. You were born into all of this."

"Not everything's about money," Colt bit out.

Jack's laugh grated across the room. "It sure as hell isn't to those who haven't earned it." He leaned forward, his palms on the desk. "Those of us that sweat blood for it have a greater respect for its value. You think this place materialized overnight? It took generations to build this estate and it'll take several more to ensure its survival."

"And you're the man to see to it, right?"

"I'm the only one that *can*." His brows rose. "What? You want to do it? Think you can waltz in here after seven years, step into Daddy's shoes and make it happen?" He shoved himself off the desk. "It doesn't work like that, Colt. You might own the place now but you're no one out there—where it counts."

Colt balled his fists. "And Margaret? She counts as no one, too? That's why you didn't even bother to deliver the news of her parents' death in person?"

Jack brushed a hand over his upper lip. "She was at school. The headmistress was with her. What else could I have done? There were important business matters that had to be tended to. Things your father worked hard for. You know as well as I do how much he would've wanted me to finish them. Remember his mantra?" His jaw hardened. *"No matter what."*

Colt's gut roiled, the taste of bile rising at the back of his throat. He eyed Jack, uncurled his fists and shook his head. "How lucky Margaret is to have you."

Jack hissed in a breath and rounded the desk. "You sanctimonious, condescending little prick." His voice rose. "Where the hell were you, huh? Cruising through every Podunk spot on the map? Riding bulls and women? You couldn't even be bothered to answer your damned phone last night when I called."

Colt flinched. Heat singed his face and chest.

"She's *your* sister." Jack scoffed. "Not mine. But I was the one left to deal with it. Hell, I couldn't get a single soul with her blood running through their veins to respond to my calls. Your grandmother's the only one I managed to reach and she's on a European tour. It took me an hour and a hefty support check to convince her to collect Margaret when she returns next month."

"Next month? Who's looking after her till then?"

A snide expression crossed Jack's face. "Should be you. Your father designated you as her legal guardian in his will."

Colt's stomach dropped. "What?"

*Legal guardian?* The old man must've overlooked that detail when he signed off on the document. There was no way Colt was fit to be any kid's guardian. Especially Meg's.

"That's got to be a mistake." He held up a hand. "There's no way… I can't—"

"I figured as much." Jack straightened. "I've already made arrangements with the school. She stays there during the week. Your father and Rachel had her picked up on weekends, though they didn't always hang around to greet her when she arrived. People are paid to do that, and God knows, it costs enough. The headmistress has agreed to board her full-time at the end of next week. Right after spring break. There's a nanny and enough staff here to meet her needs until then." He gestured to the stack of papers on the desk. "Once you sign these documents, your grandmother will take over responsibility for her.

Thank God money matters to most people. Otherwise, Margaret would end up being a worthless aggravation. As it is, money's the only thing that's going to ensure a solid future for her."

Colt's legs grew weak and his shoulders sagged.

Jack smiled, flashing bright white teeth. "Aw, buck up, boy. You'll be back to groping bulls and beauties in no time."

"That's enough."

Jen's voice, quiet but firm, sounded at Colt's back. She stood in the entrance, pulling the doors closed and fixing her eyes on Jack.

"Margaret's right down the hall," she said. "This place echoes like a museum and your voice carries."

Jack's smile morphed into a slow grin as his gaze drifted over Jen. "You must've changed course, Colt. Don't think you picked this one up in Podunk. Though I doubt you found her in Tuxedo Park, either."

Colt stiffened, his skin prickling.

Jack held out a hand. "Charmed."

Jen made no move to take it. "I'm not."

Jack's eyes flared and he cut a look at Colt. "Fiery piece of ass, is she?"

The crack as his fist met Jack's face was

enough to sharpen Colt's focus. Jen yanked at his biceps, attempting to dislodge his grip from around Jack's neck.

"Let him go, Colt." Jen's low words barely overcame the roaring in his ears.

His gut heaved on a renewed surge of pain and disgust. For his dead father. For the ambitious fool stretched across the desk beneath him. And for himself.

"Colt." Jen sobbed, her mouth moving against the skin of his neck. "*Please*. Margaret could come in. You want her to see this?"

A wave of remorse flooded him. Colt let Jack go, hanging his head.

"I might be no one out there." Colt struggled to suck in air, lungs stinging just as they did every time he conquered a bull in the arena. "But in here, I own you." His eyes burned as he glared at Jack's crumpled form. "Now get the hell out."

Jack turned over, braced his palms on the desk and struggled to a standing position. He cupped a hand over his nose. Blood seeped between his fingers, trickling over his smile and onto his tie.

"You might not have a taste for money, Colt, but you sure as hell have one for power." Jack laughed, wincing as the sound left his lips. "You're more like your father than you think."

Colt froze.

The doors closed behind Jack with a sharp click.

Jen touched his back. "Colt—"

He jerked away, moving on weak legs to the window and almost choking on the words tearing from his throat. "Margaret heard? Everything?"

"No," she said. "But more than you would've wanted her to."

And more than he'd have wanted Jen to hear, too.

Colt cringed, looking away from her faint reflection in the glass and down at the extensive grounds below him. The pristine gardens, sparkling pool and spacious tennis court were all beautiful. But barren and lifeless. Just like John W. Mead.

*You're more like your father than you think.*

Colt sucked his teeth. To hell with Jack Evans and his arrogant declarations. Colt was nothing like his father. And never would be.

"We're leaving," he growled. "Right after the funerals tomorrow."

The words were easy. They rolled off his tongue with finality. But they left a hollow in his gut. One that made him wonder if he could actually follow through.

What kind of man would leave a little girl behind? Allow her to fade into empty surroundings, forgotten and unseen?

Colt frowned, stilling his thoughts and avoiding the answer. But it whispered through his mind just the same.

Men like Jack Evans. Men like John W. Mead.

*Chapter 4*

Jen had never seen so much green in her life. It covered everything.

"Perfect." Mac, an older stable hand with a kind face and friendly voice, propped his hands on his hips. "Absolutely perfect."

"Yeah," Jen breathed.

She glanced around, taking in the sprawling acres of lush grass and the thick lines of trees forming a boundary on both sides of the wide pasture. If there was ever a paradise for horses, the riding grounds on the Mead estate were it.

"He fast?"

Jen glanced at Mac, squinting through the sharp rays of late afternoon sunlight. "What?"

"Your horse." He jerked his chin toward the field where Diamond had been frolicking for the past hour, pearl hide flashing through a sea of green. "He's a fine specimen. But is he fast?"

She cocked a brow and grinned. "What do you think?"

Mac chuckled, his leathery cheeks lifting and white teeth gleaming. "I think if we let those pampered ponies out of the stable, he'd trample 'em just on principle."

Jen laughed with him, dropping her head back and soaking up the fading warmth of the day. It'd been nice to get out of that marbled mansion for a few hours. Colt's father's estate was void of any true warmth. Only cold corners and empty hallways could be found in that monster of a house.

After that arrogant jerk Jack Evans had left, Colt had gathered up their luggage and led her up another massive staircase to the third floor, where the guest rooms were located. They'd stowed their bags in their bedrooms and Colt had immediately left to seek out Margaret. But Margaret hadn't responded to any of his attempts at conversation. She'd just looked him over with narrowed eyes, then retreated to her room.

Colt, more stoic than ever, had excused himself and holed up in his father's study. Jen had tried to persuade him to join her outside, but he'd continued to pore over the guardianship papers Jack Evans had prepared, lingering over each page before moving grimly to the next.

Jen glanced back at the long path up to the mansion. Neither Colt nor Margaret had come outside all day. Ms. Parks had insisted Margaret not be disturbed, and the door to the girl's bedroom had remained shut for hours. Which was a shame. Fresh air and warm sunshine were the best antidotes for pain.

"Mr. and Mrs. Mead never really cared for riding," Mac said, a note of disgust in his tone. "Or the horses, for that matter. They just liked the idea of owning them."

"What about Margaret?" Jen asked. "She never rides?"

"Not since—"

"Never."

Jen spun to find Margaret standing behind them. She'd traded her school uniform for a white skirt and blue blouse, but still wore her hot-pink shoes. Her long hair fell in loose waves around her face, but her expression remained blank.

"You should come in now," Margaret said. "Dinner is being served."

Jen's stomach growled at the mention of food. She'd stayed outside so long she'd missed lunch. "Sounds good." She smiled. "Thank you for telling me, Margaret."

"Ms. Parks said it's important to personally invite guests to the dinner table." She shrugged. "Even if you weren't expecting them. It's the polite thing to do and it's never polite to be late."

Margaret hesitated for a moment, her chestnut eyes lingering on Diamond, then turned and left.

Jen released a bitter laugh. "Ms. Parks sounds like a pretty tough customer."

"I don't know," Mac said. "She's a lot better than the last four nannies that little girl's had."

*"Four?"* Jen shook her head. "Why so many?"

"Mrs. Mead was real particular about who she kept around. She always found something she didn't like about them." Mac grimaced. "Usually right after they'd suggest she pay more attention to her daughter."

He squinted, staring at Diamond in the distance. "Imogene Holden was the child's first nanny. Was with her from birth. She was

Margaret's favorite. Took Margaret out for her first ride." He dragged a hand across the back of his neck. "They weren't out long before the horse spooked. Took off so fast Imogene couldn't catch hold of it. Margaret was thrown. Got hurt pretty bad."

"And now she doesn't trust them," Jen murmured.

Mac nodded. "Imogene was fired right after. That kid loved Imogene something fierce. She cried for days after she left. Shed a lot more tears over that nanny than she has for her own parents, that's for sure." His features fell and his voice deepened. "Not that anyone can blame her for that."

Mac's hunched shoulders and defeated expression proved the loss of Imogene had been a cruel blow to others besides Margaret. So strange that a place equipped with every material comfort imaginable would be filled with an equal amount of pain. Was no one happy here?

"Well," Jen whispered, clearing her throat. "I guess it's time for me to go in. Would you mind tucking Diamond in for the night? I'd really appreciate it."

"No problem," he said, straightening with a smile. "Any time."

Jen made her way up the winding stone path to the main entrance. A housekeeper met her at the door, ushering her inside with rapid waves of her hands and leading her quickly down several hallways to a formal dining room.

"Good evening, Ms. Taylor." Ms. Parks sat on one side of a long cherry table, Margaret seated at her side. "We were beginning to wonder if you'd make it."

Colt rose from his position at the head of the table and tugged out the high-backed chair to his left. "We weren't aware there was a schedule," he said in a firm voice.

Jen winced. The circles under Colt's eyes had darkened and new lines of strain were etched in his expression. His formal gesture only added to his distant demeanor.

"I'm sorry I kept everyone waiting," she said, unable to stop herself from squeezing his hand before taking her seat. "When we're on the road, Colt and I don't have time to stand on ceremony. We just grab and go. Right?"

The corners of his mouth tipped up slightly as he sat. "Yeah."

Jen's chest constricted. Grief was taking a toll on him and this place was only intensifying it. Fine friend she was being. Nothing she'd done so far had helped ease his pain.

She glanced around the room and shifted uncomfortably in her chair. A large, crystal chandelier hung above from the center of a ceiling mural. Ornate floral arrangements and elegant place settings were strategically arranged on the polished cherry table.

Jen flexed her fingers to shake off a fresh surge of anxiety, then tugged the napkin ring from the cloth in the center of her plate. "So," she said, settling the napkin in her lap, "what's on the menu?"

Ms. Parks and Margaret exchanged glances, and after an encouraging nod from her nanny, Margaret recited, "Chilled scallops with saffron mayonnaise, asparagus and buttered leeks and radishes."

Jen suppressed a shudder. "That sounds… different."

It smelled different, too. And judging from the curl of Colt's upper lip, he was just as impressed with the sparsely covered plate that appeared in front of him as she was. The housekeeper filled their crystal glasses with water and left to retrieve sliced lemon at Ms. Parks's request.

"Please eat, Margaret." The nanny speared a scallop with her fork and dipped it in the yellow sauce.

Margaret wasn't as adept. Her scallop fell off the fork and plopped into the sauce bowl, splattering yellow drops onto the white place setting. She fished around for a few seconds with her fork, but when Ms. Parks turned her head, she retrieved it with her fingers and slipped it in her mouth quickly.

One grimace and hard swallow later, Margaret placed her fork on the table and sat back. Colt followed suit, pushing his plate away with the tip of his finger and casting tired eyes over his sister.

Ms. Parks sighed, forehead creasing. "Margaret, you need to eat."

Jen frowned. Colt needed to eat, too. But the meal in front of them was about as appetizing as baked rubber.

The housekeeper returned, placing a small plate of lemon wedges on the table near Ms. Parks. "May I bring you anything, Mr. Mead?"

Colt shook his head. "No, thanks."

Jen leaned forward, halting the housekeeper's exit with a raised hand. "I could use something, please." She smiled. "I'm sorry—what's your name?"

The woman hesitated, darting glances at Ms. Parks and licking her lips. "Nancy."

"Do you happen to have any peanut butter, Nancy?"

She tilted her head. "Yes, ma'am, we do."

"Could you bring it, please? And honey. Do you have honey?"

"Yes, ma'am. How would you like it?"

Jen shrugged. "Just a jar of both would be fine. And some bread. I'd like to fix it up myself."

The housekeeper nodded, then left, the fading swish of her slacks filling the silent room.

Margaret sat up, confusion clouding her features. "Aren't you supposed to eat jelly with peanut butter?"

Jen's smile widened. "That's the go-to for most people. But I found something better growing up."

She picked up her plate of scallops and unappealing vegetables, then dumped them on top of Colt's.

Ms. Parks's eyes widened. "There's no point in making a mess. If you need another plate, we'll happily provide one for you."

"Nah." Jen met Colt's eyes, her belly fluttering at the amusement brightening his dark expression. "Wouldn't want to dirty up more dishes than necessary."

The housekeeper returned, placing the requested items on the table. Jen dipped out a hefty portion of peanut butter and honey, plopped them onto her plate and stirred them together.

"When I was in elementary school," Jen said, "the lunchroom lady, Mrs. Shirley, would sneak me a special sandwich every Wednesday. It was always white bread with this thick, sweet stuff in the middle that I loved. I knew peanut butter was in it, but it took me a while to figure out what the sweet stuff was." She picked up a clean spoon and scooped up a dollop of the mixture. "Turned out it was honey. But you have to combine just the right amounts to get the same taste."

Ms. Parks's left eyebrow lifted almost to her hairline. "This was in public school, I imagine?"

"Yep." Jen held the loaded spoon out to Meg. "There's a lot more to learn in public school than just academics." She waited as Meg took the spoon and placed it gingerly in her mouth. "I learned that lunchroom ladies are moms, sisters and daughters, too. That most teachers care about other people's children as if they were their own. And that some kids you'd never thought you'd like can end up being the best friends you ever had."

Margaret's mouth curved up and she said, "Wis is uh beft swuff evah."

"Margaret," Ms. Parks gasped. "Don't speak with your mouth full."

"Buh i' is," Margaret said, lifting the spoon in an obvious request for more.

Colt laughed, picked up his spoon and held it out, as well. The deep rumble tingled over Jen's skin, dancing in her chest and bringing a wet sheen to her eyes. She blinked rapidly, filled both their spoons, then her own, and even offered one to Ms. Parks.

"No, thank you."

"Oh, come on," Jen teased. "Just try it."

Surprisingly, she did. The sound of pleasure that followed indicated she approved.

The next few minutes passed in companionable silence as they assembled sandwiches and filled their bellies. Colt ate three, and when Margaret asked for a second one, he put his half-eaten fourth sandwich aside to make her another.

"Thank you," she murmured, taking the sandwich from him with a gooey, crumb-laden smile.

"You're welcome." Colt's grin couldn't get any wider.

Jen sneaked her napkin to her cheek and

wiped her eyes before anyone noticed. Such a foolish thing to do—tearing up like a baby when Colt and Margaret were the ones who needed a good cry.

"All right, Margaret," Ms. Parks said, standing. "It's time for homework then bed."

"But I want another—"

"You've had two and that's quite enough for a little girl." She ushered Margaret from her chair.

"If she wants to stay and have another sandwich, she can." Colt's tone hardened as he watched Margaret trudge slowly across the room.

"It's up to you, of course," Ms. Parks said. "But considering the long day she'll have tomorrow, I think it's best that she get a good night's rest. Don't you?"

Colt's expression fell at the reminder of the funerals. He nodded.

Ms. Parks waited until Margaret was out of earshot, then said, "I understand what you're both trying to do and no one appreciates it more than me. That's the first genuine smile Margaret's had in ages." She bit her lip and lowered her voice. "I'm paid to supervise and advise Margaret. Not love her. But I do. And I can't, in any good conscience, step aside and allow you to fill her heart with hopes of things that will never happen."

"I have every right to visit Margaret," Colt said. "I'm her brother."

"In name only." Ms. Parks fidgeted. "Forgive me, but I wasn't under the impression that you planned to stay."

Colt released a ragged breath, his eyes dropping.

"Please understand," Ms. Parks continued. "None of what you're teaching Margaret right now will do her any good in the life she'll soon lead. It will only be a disservice to her. As I'm sure you already know." She hesitated, then whispered on her departure, "I'm sorry, Mr. Mead. I truly am."

Colt dragged his hand over his face then slid his palm around to knead the back of his neck. "I think it's time to call it a day."

His voice sounded strange. Heavy and unfamiliar, as though it belonged to a different man.

"Colt." Jen wrapped her fingers gently around his forearm. "I'm here if you want to talk. It might help if—"

"I'm tired." He pulled away and stood, tossing his napkin on the table. "Good night."

He ambled out, his steps slow and defeated.

Wet heat streaked down Jen's cheeks. She didn't bother to wipe her face. Just let the steady stream continue. She'd cried more in the past twenty-four hours than she had in three years put together. And Colt had yet to shed a tear.

Jen pushed her chair back and stood, taking in the empty room around her. It was impossible to imagine Colt or Margaret having a good childhood here. The loneliness of the place hung on them like a thick shroud, and it was beginning to fall over her, as well.

This wasn't a home. And no matter how much her heart bled for him, Colt wasn't hers. The sooner she put this weekend behind her and returned to the circuit, the better.

There wasn't a wet eye in the church. Not a single tear was shed during the funeral, and Colt wasn't surprised. That was the way John W. Mead wanted things done in his world.

"John Mead will be missed as much for his philanthropy as for his strength of spirit." The preacher paused, shifting behind the pulpit and sweeping his gentle eyes over the first pew. "Those who knew him best can be proud of his generosity to others. So many have benefited from John's charity and goodwill."

Colt bit back a scoff. His father's checks were easy to cut, always signed by secretaries. They allowed for greater tax write-offs. And no one, including his family, had ever really known John W. Mead. He never let anyone close enough.

But there was no need to split hairs at this point. They'd already sat through an hour of services for Rachel, and were on the second one for his father. Besides himself and Margaret, Jen and Ms. Parks were the only people seated in the family pew. And the strain of the day was beginning to take its toll.

He dropped his head and gripped the edge of his seat, the rough upholstery of the pew abrading his fingertips. Margaret's pale hand, one-third the size of his, lay flat on the seat beside his thigh and shook slightly.

A heavy weight pressed on Colt's chest. He ached to reach out, place his palm over the back of her small one and squeeze. To still her nerves with solid strength and help her feel less alone.

Because that was exactly what she was. Alone. With no knowledge of how much her gurgling toddler laugh had comforted him all those years ago. Or how relieved he'd always been as a teenager to see her at the end of each school day. Her rambunctious demeanor had been the only bright spot in that dark mansion.

*I don't remember.*

Meg's—*Margaret's*—words returned, dropping like a stone into his gut. She didn't remember him and he wouldn't be around long enough to remind her. He'd packed his bags first thing this morning, loaded the truck and mapped out the fastest route back to the circuit. His plan hinged on driving away the moment the funerals ended.

Only he hadn't counted on the news he'd received from Tammy when she'd called to check on him.

"Colt." Jen's soft lips brushed his ear as she tugged gently at his wrist.

He glanced up, taking in her worried expression, then noticed everyone was standing. Clearing his throat, he released his hold on the pew and stood. Jen took his hand in hers, then wrapped her free one around his biceps, squeezing firmly.

The gesture was calm and kind. An act of one friend supporting another. But it reignited all sorts of emotions within him, ones he'd only ever felt with Jen. The kind he couldn't define or understand.

It'd be so easy to lean into her. To pass this pressing weight to her and absorb every bit of supportive comfort she offered. But he couldn't. Not when Margaret stood silent at his side, expression empty and posture aloof. An exact replica of his father's demeanor, void of any traces of the affectionate girl Colt once knew.

The pallbearers gathered around the caskets and the procession began. Another hour passed at the cemetery. By the time Colt's small group exited the limo and climbed the steep front steps of the Mead estate, his sister had lost her last bit of color. She fiddled with the black bow at her waist as she followed Ms. Parks across the foyer toward the hall.

"Margaret." Colt struggled to force her name past his constricted throat, the syllables echoing off the marble walls. "Would you like to sit with me for a while?" He shrugged, his tense shoulders screaming in protest. "Or we could take a walk?"

She stopped, then glanced over her shoulder, blond curls and thick lashes drooping. "Ms. Parks said you're probably leaving soon. Are you?"

Colt hesitated, glancing at Jen, who stood by the closed doors of the front entrance. She looked at him sadly but pointedly.

His body sagged and he moved to the window, staring out at the long driveway and trying to still the trembling in his limbs. "Yeah."

"Then we won't have time to, will we?" Margaret's quiet voice barely reached him.

Time. That's what it all amounted to. The hours it took to make the drive here. The days he'd sacrificed to attend the funerals. And the years of obligation that would pile up if the papers sitting on his father's desk remained unsigned.

Colt dug his fingertips into the windowsill, pressing hard against the wood until his nail beds turned red. Taking responsibility for Margaret on a permanent basis was out of the question. There was no room in his life for a kid and he didn't have the first clue how to raise one.

But how could he walk away again with no attempt at reconciliation? Remain as much a stranger to his sister as John W. Mead had been to him? A relative in name only?

Each one of Margaret's fading footsteps ripped another hole in Colt's chest. A familiar ache began to seep from the pit of his gut, the kind he'd felt ever since he'd left her behind seven years ago. It coursed through his veins, stealing his breath.

"I can make the time." He froze, unable to believe the declaration had left his mouth.

"She's gone, Colt." Jen stepped to his side and rubbed his arm. "It may be for the best, anyway. It's a long drive to the next competition, and if we don't leave soon, we won't make it."

"I need to stay with Margaret. Just for a little while longer." He reached up, stilling Jen's hand and peering down at her. "What if you sat the next race out? Or two or three, for that matter?"

Her dark eyes clouded with confusion. "What are you talking about?"

He drew in a deep breath and took her hands in his. "I spoke to Tammy this morning. Checked the stats. You're ranking eighth."

Jen's brows rose, pink lips curving slightly. "Eighth?"

He nodded. "Right now, you're qualifying for Finals. You and Tammy both. She won last night and is ranking ninth, right behind you and well above the top fifteen cut for Vegas."

"Vegas?" Jen whispered.

"Vegas, Red." He licked his lips. "You can afford to take a break." Her expression dimmed and he held up a palm. "Margaret's school is on spring vacation and she'll be alone until classes start back up if I don't stay with her. It'd just be for a week."

"One week?" Jen frowned. "This trip was only supposed to be for a couple of days, Colt. That's all Tammy asked me for and that's all I promised."

"I know. But I'm the one doing the asking now." He put his shoulders back and forged ahead. "I might've taken care of Tammy when I got out of here seven years ago, but by doing that, I left Margaret behind. That guilt has followed me for a long time. I don't want that feeling hanging on me again. I need to get rid of it."

Jen sighed, her expression gentle. "But how would a week help? Don't you think it'll be harder for you to leave her after another week than it would now?"

A strange feeling of unease moved over him. Colt dismissed it, shaking his head and firming his features.

"No," he said. "It won't. I know I'm not fit to take care of her full-time. Would never want to. But I can be here for her now. I can help her through all of this and show her another way to live."

"Colt—"

"I can give her better memories. Ones she

can carry with her when she moves on. That way when she comes of age, she can choose for herself which life she wants to lead. Like I did seven years ago." He stepped closer, trying to lighten the pleading note in his voice. "I can't do it on my own, though. I need your help."

"I don't know how I'd be of any help. I barely know her."

"That doesn't matter. You've made more headway with her in one day than a nanny who's been with her for months. You proved it last night, pulling that smile from her. Hell, Ms. Parks said so herself."

Jen drew back, shaking her head. "One smile doesn't make me an expert on kids. And this place isn't good for anyone. I can't stay here any longer, Colt."

"You won't." He firmed his tone. "We'll leave here today just as planned."

"And go where?" She splayed her hands. "You can't wander from motel to motel like you normally do, not with a nine-year-old in tow."

"I'll take care of that. I'll call in a favor."

"This is… I'm sorry, but I can't. I've got to get back to the circuit. A weekend was one thing, but a whole week—"

"You're ranking so high right now, you've got plenty of cushion. It'll take the rest of 'em that long just to catch up with you."

Jen laughed, the sound abrupt and derisive. "I doubt that."

"Seven days, tops," he insisted. "Diamond will get a well-deserved break. You'll have extra time to train. And Margaret and I will be able to get to know each other again. That way she'll feel comfortable coming to me in the future if she ever needs me." He moved close, cradling Jen's face with his palms. "This is me asking. Not Tammy. I need your help and I could really use a friend right now."

The curves of her cheeks blushed beneath his thumbs and her lush lips parted on a shaky inhalation. Her eyes met his and softened.

His throat burned. Damn, he was begging. But it didn't prevent him from whispering, "Please, Red."

Her full lashes fluttered shut as she blew out a heavy breath. "Only for one week. If my ranking drops before then, you have to promise you'll get me and Diamond back to the circuit—no matter what." She opened her eyes, expression determined. "That's a non-negotiable."

"You got it." He pressed a kiss to her forehead then stepped back quickly, ignoring the pleasurable sensation in his belly and the sudden desire to hold on to her.

Jen looked away. Her drawn expression indicated regret had already set in.

Colt flexed his fingers to ease the ache running down his arms and choked down the words fighting their way up his throat. The ones urging him to take it back. To pack up and get out while he could. Instead, he dragged his phone from his pocket and dialed. It rang twice before someone answered.

"Well, hell," a deep voice said with a chuckle. "Must be my lucky day, hearing from you."

Colt managed a smile. "Dom." Dominic Slade. A former bull rider. Known as champion to the world, though Colt knew him as best friend. A good man. One Colt trusted above any other. "Got time for an old friend?"

"Of course." Dominic's laughter faded. "You all right, man?"

"Yeah." Colt dragged in a breath and steadied his voice. "I need a favor."

Dominic responded immediately. "You name it."

# Chapter 5

"Are you sure you want to do this?"

Jen winced, pressed the cell phone closer to her ear and sneaked a glance at Colt in the driver's seat. He cut his eyes her way briefly, then refocused on the road. A quick peek in the rearview mirror revealed Margaret sleeping soundly in the back of the extended cab, just as she had since leaving the Mead estate hours earlier. Thank goodness.

Tammy's voice was pitched higher as it came across the line. "You're ranking eighth. That's not a given for Finals this early," she stressed. "There's still months to go before we officially make the cut, and you can't sit on the sidelines and expect to hold your position."

Jen rubbed her forehead, feeling as though it was midnight rather than four in the afternoon. "I know. But it's only for seven days."

"Seven days?" Tammy's voice was still strained. "Might as well be seven years. Things move so fast out here, you'll fall behind before you know it." Her tone lowered. "This is my fault. I should never have talked you into going in the first place. That's why you feel like you have to do this."

"That's not true," Jen whispered, turning to look out the passenger window.

The landscape passed by in a blur of green, wide fields separated by thick woods stretching endlessly. Each mile took them deeper into Georgia country and away from the circuit.

Why *had* she agreed to Colt's request?

Tammy sighed. "How's Colt doing?"

Jen stole a glance at him. His knuckles turned white around the steering wheel and he blinked slowly, his eyes heavy.

Jen's chest ached. Now she remembered why she'd given in.

"Okay, I guess," she murmured. "It's going to take some time."

"I'm glad you're there for him," Tammy said. "And for Margaret. I really am. I just worry that if you don't get back soon, you won't make the cut. You've worked so hard for so long, Jen. I'd hate for you to..."

Jen closed her eyes briefly, her own fears finishing Tammy's sentence.

*I'd hate for you to lose it all.* End up a small-town nothing like everyone predicted, mopping the floor of The Greasy Spoon every day and surviving off a few dollars' worth of tips. Living in a cramped house filled with more hungry mouths than working hands. Exactly like Jen's mother, Nora, had.

Nora Taylor, a widow and overworked waitress, had dismissed her daughter's ambition to become a world champion barrel racer despite Jen's repeated success at rodeos near their hometown. Her outlook on life was as weary and bleak as the abandoned house rotting next to theirs.

*It's dangerous, Jen. Not to mention improper. Prancing around an arena, rubbing shoulders with sweaty cowboys. Since you're not going to college, the best thing for you is to find a good man and settle down. Start a family.*

Jen scoffed. *Hogwash.* "I'm coming back

in one week." She smiled. "You better stay on your toes if you plan to keep up. Diamond and I always burn brighter after a good rest."

Tammy laughed, but the joyful sound faded quickly. "Take care of them."

"I will." Jen disconnected the call and tucked her cell phone back in her pocket.

"Tammy meeting us later?" Colt asked.

Jen shook her head. "She's already lined up more runs with Karla. Says they've paid entry fees for three competitions, started the drive yesterday and are halfway there. She can't afford to dip out now. It'd put Karla in a bad position."

She cringed. The kind of position she'd left Tammy in when she'd decided to stay behind with Colt.

Colt's big hand settled over hers and squeezed, his blue eyes weary. "We'll be back before you know it, Red."

"We're not going to worry about that at the moment," Jen said, covering his hand with her free one. "Right now, we're taking a break. One you and Margaret desperately need."

His big body shifted and he tugged his hand away, reaching up and squeezing her shoulder. He returned his attention to the road, easing across a bumpy set of railroad tracks, then accelerating down the highway.

Jen inhaled, relishing the spicy scent of his aftershave and the warmth his touch had left on her skin. It was easier to travel with him when Tammy was around. Tammy's cheerful chatter helped take the focus off Colt's charisma. But Jen didn't have that luxury on this trip.

Colt's biceps brushed her arm as he maneuvered another turn, causing her belly to flip over. She placed her hands in her lap and tamped down the urge to scoot closer and press against him.

It was ridiculous, really. Indulging this attraction she had to him. She tried to convince herself that any man with Colt's good looks and muscular frame would stir the same desire. They were friends. That was all he wanted. Nothing more.

A sleepy sigh emerged from the back of the cab. Jen glanced over her shoulder. Margaret had sat upright in her seat during the first half of the journey, but exhaustion had finally taken over. She was now slumped against the window, her shiny hair falling forward, hiding her face. A few strands lifted and fell as she breathed.

A lump formed in Jen's throat at the sight. After arranging a place for them to stay, Colt had gently explained to his little sister that he needed a break, a vacation of sorts, and that he'd like her to come with him.

Ms. Parks had disapproved and Margaret hadn't responded much one way or the other. But after a half hour of coaxing from Colt, they'd given in to his declaration that he wasn't leaving without Margaret, and gone upstairs to pack a bag. Jen had offered to help, but Margaret declined in a formal manner that was much too mature for any nine-year-old. Especially one who had to be hurting as much as she was.

Jen bit her lip now and tried her best to make out Margaret's face through the fall of her curls. The girl shared the same blond shade of hair as Colt. The brief glimpse Jen had had of her smile last night proved that was another similarity the siblings shared. Jen just wasn't sure she'd ever see her smile again.

Her arms ached to wrap around Margaret and hug her. To offer comfort in some small way. But she knew the attempt would be refused. Margaret might have been provided for in every other way, but she'd been neglected in the most important respect. Being loved. And noticed.

Jen's heart squeezed. Margaret was such a sad, beautiful girl—

Vibrating snorts rang out. Margaret's head shifted against the foggy window, her hair slipping back and her small mouth falling open on a massive snore. A raucous chorus began, thundering against the roof and filling the cab. For the sixth time in the last hour.

Jen cringed, sharing a pained glance with Colt. Three hours ago, Margaret's snores had been cute and endearing. Two hours ago, they'd become aggravating. Now they were excruciating.

Jen's head pounded. Good grief, she couldn't wait to get out of this stuffy truck, collapse onto a bed and savor some silence. Alone.

Ten snore-filled minutes later, Colt turned onto a long dirt drive, and a familiar wooden sign appeared ahead. Jen would recognize the rustic corners and rich brown of it anywhere. She'd driven past it with Colt several times over the past couple of years, to visit friends from the rodeo circuit.

Raintree Ranch. They'd finally made it. Privacy, silence and sleep were just up ahead inside the white, multistoried main house.

Margaret's rhythmic snorts stopped as the truck bounced over a rough patch of road. Jen swiveled, to find her sweeping her hair back from her face and blinking sleepy eyes at the view outside her window.

"A ranch?" Margaret asked as the truck eased past the sign. "You said we were taking a vacation."

Colt glanced in the rearview mirror, his smile strained. "We are. Raintree's the best guest ranch in Georgia. There are lots of fun things to do. There's a pool, game room and a pond with paddleboats. And there are a couple boys here around your age to play with. I'll take you fishing one day this week. You'll love it, Meg."

Her expression fell. "It's Margaret," she whispered.

"I'm sorry." Colt shifted uncomfortably, cheeks reddening. "Margaret."

Margaret turned away and stared at the line of white fencing sweeping by. The air grew thick and heavy inside the cab.

Jen hit a button on the passenger door and the window slid down with a whisper, letting in a warm breeze. She stuck her head out, inhaled and pulled in a lungful of sweet spring air. The chirp of crickets and low notes of bullfrogs rushed into the cab; the late afternoon hour and misty fog coaxed songs from the ranch wildlife.

She soaked it up. The tension between her shoulder blades eased and the throbbing at her temples lessened. Just the wide green fields speckled with grazing horses were enough to lift her spirits.

The trailer squeaked as the truck dipped into a pothole. Jen lowered her cheek to the silver windowsill trim and looked back, catching a glimpse of Diamond's white mane through the slats of the trailer.

She hadn't ridden him in two days. Neither one of them had felt the whip of wind striking their face in ages. Or smelled the rich, earthy aroma of dirt kicking up from beneath them. And she was surprised by how eager she was to ride outside an arena rather than in one.

"Not long now, boy," she whispered. "We can both stretch our legs soon. I'll have you back in shape in no time."

"What?"

Jen pushed herself off the door and straightened, glancing at Colt. His brow was furrowed.

"Just telling Diamond I'm gonna let him

out soon. We're anxious to stretch a bit. Maybe hit up some training in the morning."

Colt nodded. She turned back to the window, an excited buzz spreading through her veins. Training. One benefit to taking a break was the opportunity to hone her racing skills. She and Diamond would be better than ever when they returned to competition.

Jen closed her eyes and savored the thrills chasing through her blood. Eighth overall. The Thomas & Mack. *Vegas*.

"There's Dom." Colt perked up, a pleased note entering his voice.

A tall, broad-shouldered man stood at the end of the driveway, a black Stetson on his head and dimpled smile on his face.

Colt cut the engine, jumped out and started toward him. The man met him halfway, tugging him forward for a brief hug and strong clap on the back. When they broke apart, Jen she could see that they were talking.

Before long, Colt nodded and motioned toward the truck.

"Who's he?"

Jen swiveled, glancing back at Margaret. "Dominic Slade. He used to ride bulls with your brother. He co-owns this ranch with his father, Pop, and his brother, Logan." She smiled. "They're good people. And they're all anxious to meet you."

Margaret's brown eyes drifted over Jen's shoulder and she leaned forward, squinting up at the main house. "It looks small."

Jen reassessed the building. The wide front porch, large double door entrance and multi-leveled structure was anything but small. It'd grown over the last two years with renovations and the addition of more guest wings. But she supposed it paled in comparison to what Margaret was used to.

"There's plenty of room." Jen stretched her legs and grinned. *Rooms.* One, in particular. With a large bed, en suite bathroom and plenty of sleep-inducing silence. All for her. *Hallelujah!* "Come on. I'll help you get your bag."

Jen had just hefted Margaret's bag from the bed of the truck when the front door slammed and feet pounded down the front steps. Two blond boys loped across the lawn, shouting greetings to "Mr. Colt" and high-fiving him.

Jen smiled and set the bag on the ground. "That's Kayden and Jayden, Dominic's twin nephews. The boys Colt told you about. They oughta be fun to hang out with, don't you think?"

Margaret tucked a curl behind her ear and ran a hand over her plaid skirt. "They live here all the time? With their mom and dad?"

Jen's smile slipped. "The boys live here, yes. With Dominic and his wife, Cissy."

She hesitated, unsure of how much to share. Kayden and Jayden had lost their mother several years ago to cancer. Their father planned on giving them up for adoption, but their aunt Cissy had taken them in. After finding Cissy and the boys stranded in a broken-down car, Dominic had brought the trio to Raintree and they'd eventually become a family.

Jen shrugged, thinking it best to keep the darker details of the boys' journey to herself. It might help soothe Margaret's grief to know she wasn't alone in her pain, but it could backfire just as easily. Jen didn't want to add more negativity to Margaret's world at such a difficult time. Besides, they were here to help her heal. The brighter the thoughts, the better.

"The boys have baby sisters, too. They'd be about, oh…" Jen squinted, counting the months "…almost two years old now." She waved at Dominic. "Hey, Dom. It's good to see you."

He flashed a dimpled grin and called out, "Back atcha, Red. It's great to have you here."

Jen eased to the front of the truck and motioned for Margaret to follow. "Come on. I'll introduce you."

The little girl stepped forward, but her hot-pink tennis shoe halted in midair over the dirt.

Jen followed Margaret's stare. The boys had left Colt and now stood stock-still, side by side, a few feet away, big blue eyes fixed on Margaret. Their hushed voices carried.

"Another girl?" Kayden shared a frown with his brother. "Ain't we got enough of those around here?"

Jayden harrumphed, crossing his arms over his chest. "I know. Thought it was gonna be a boy." He shook his head. "That messes up all our plans."

Great. Preadolescent disdain for the opposite sex. A fantastic first impression.

Jen smiled. "Aw, now. Y'all cut that out, boys. I'm a girl, too. Aren't you happy to see me?" She laughed at their eager nods, dropped to her knees and spread her arms. "Then get your cute tails over here and show Miss Jen some love."

They flashed crooked grins and sprinted

over, barreling into her and wrapping their arms around her neck. They'd grown since she last saw them, Kayden a good three inches and Jayden at least two. They'd be almost nine now.

"You bring Diamond, Miss Jen?" Kayden asked, pecking a kiss to her cheek.

"I sure did." She jerked her chin toward the trailer behind them. "Go tell him hi. He's been cooped up a long time and would appreciate the company."

Kayden released her and headed for the trailer, his step slowing as he passed Margaret. Their eyes met and then drifted down the length of each other. Kayden's attention returned to her blond curls, and he blushed.

Jen stifled a laugh and stood. "You know, it's usually routine to at least say hello when you meet someone new."

Kayden shrugged a shoulder. "Hey."

"Hello." Margaret held out a hand. "I'm Margaret Mead."

Kayden's nose wrinkled. He studied her outstretched hand for a moment before shaking it awkwardly. "I'm Kayden." He nodded toward his brother. "That's Jayden."

"It's nice to meet you," Margaret said.

Kayden eyed her flashy sneakers. "Me and

Jayden race a lot. He's fast but I'm faster." His head tilted. "You ever race?"

"No."

"You build forts?"

"Uh-uh."

"Shoot BB guns?"

Margaret shook her head, her expression appalled.

Kayden sighed. "Then what do you do?"

Jayden snorted. "She paints her toes and stuff." He walked over, shoving his brother toward the trailer. "Come on. Let's pet Diamond."

Attention diverted, Kayden sauntered over to the trailer with his twin. They climbed up on the tires, slipped their hands through the open window and patted Diamond, praising him. Margaret took a hesitant step toward them, but froze when Diamond shifted, hooves clanking on the bed of the trailer. She looked at the boys' T-shirts, jeans and boots, then lowered her head and picked at her silk blouse.

Jen stepped close and placed a hand on her shoulder. "You're welcome to pet Diamond, too, if you'd like."

Her head shot up, face pale and tone tense. "I don't want to."

The boys' hands stilled and they glanced over their shoulders, examining Margaret, who flushed and tilted her chin higher.

"No, thank you." She glanced at the twins out of the corner of her eyes. "I'd prefer to go inside and recuperate. It was a long trip."

Kayden hopped off the trailer and settled his hands on his hips. "She talks funny."

Margaret's brown eyes flashed.

"Dresses funny, too," Jayden said, climbing down.

"That's enough, boys." Jen stepped between them when she saw Margaret's chin begin to wobble. "I think your aunt Cissy would expect you to be more polite to a guest."

They both dropped their heads, studying the scuffed toes of their boots.

Margaret's eyes filled to the brim and she spun away, snatching at the handle of one of her bags. She couldn't manage to lift it so she dragged it through the dirt behind her instead.

"What's going on here?" Dominic rounded the truck and cast a stern eye on the boys.

They squirmed and Kayden peeked up from beneath his lashes. "Sorry, Uncle Dominic."

"Yeah. Me, too," Jayden added.

"Wait, Margaret." Colt bent and reached for her bag. "Let me get that."

"No, thank you." His sister scrubbed the back of her hand over her cheeks and stomped off, dragging the case behind her. "I can do it myself."

Colt frowned as she struggled across the lawn to the porch steps, her bulky bag flattening the lush blades of grass along the way. His shoulders sagged and the shadows darkening his expression deepened.

Jen cringed. Colt wanted so badly for this to work. For this visit to restore his relationship with Margaret. But the outlook was grim and she didn't have the heart to tell him.

She glanced up at the large house and sighed. Margaret had a point, though. It was past time for some private recuperation. She and Colt both needed it.

"After I unload Diamond, why don't we go in, too?" Jen asked, nodding at Colt. "Get settled in our rooms and turn in early? I think we could use some rest."

"Yeah." Dominic cleared his throat and shifted his stance. "About that."

Jen's eyes shot to his face. His grin widened.

"We had a bigger crowd than I expected.

There's only one guest room available." Dominic held up a hand. "But I don't consider y'all guests, anyway. You're both family. Colt's chosen to take the smaller guest room and I'm setting you up in a larger family room in the main house."

"That sounds great. Thanks." Jen shrugged and smiled. "Where's Margaret staying? Family floor, too?"

Dominic nodded. "Yep. With you."

Jen's smile froze, a nervous tick forming in the corner of her eye. "Great."

Nothing was going according to Colt's plan. Barely twenty-four hours after arriving at Raintree, he was beginning to believe he'd made a grave mistake.

He knuckled his hat higher on his forehead and wiped the sweat from his brow. At his side stood Margaret, squinting against the sun's glare and wringing her skirt with both hands. They watched as Jen rode Diamond across the grassy field in front of them.

Though he tried to avoid it, Colt found himself focusing on the graceful way Jen moved with the horse. Each tap of her heel drew his eyes to the curves of her legs and every lift of her wavy hair in the breeze made him long to run his fingers through the fiery strands.

He shoved his hands in his pockets, stilling the desire stirring within him. His attention should be on Margaret right now. Not on Jen.

"Diamond's big but he's gentle," Jen called, nudging the quarter horse with her heels and walking him farther out. "See, Margaret? He'll do anything I ask."

Colt's sister looked down and edged closer to the fence. Wisps of hair stuck to her sweaty cheeks and her fair skin had turned red. The short-sleeved blouse and knee-length skirt she wore did little to block the strong afternoon rays.

From what Colt had gathered at the mansion, she spent a lot of time indoors. And she'd remained outside for the majority of her first day at Raintree. He hadn't even thought about a hat or sunscreen. He'd been too busy thinking about Jen.

Colt frowned. *Strike one for big brother.*

"You don't have to ride if you don't want to," he said. "It was just an idea."

One of many he'd had that failed. And one Jen had tried to talk him out of. He glanced at Jen and shook his head.

No need to drag this out. Margaret had

made it clear all day that she wasn't interested in anything other than holing up in the guest room. She'd rejected every suggestion he'd made for entertainment, offering either a polite excuse or silent refusal.

"It's okay, Margaret." Jen threw her leg over Diamond's back and hopped down, her boots sloshing on the muddy ground as she led the horse toward them.

It had rained hard last night after they'd retired. Rained for three hours. Colt had counted. Unable to sleep, he'd slumped in a chair by the window and listened to it pound the roof. Had even been grateful for it at the time. The sharp cracks of thunder and blinding flashes of lightning had silenced his thoughts. Ones that involved fears of failing Margaret and guilt over keeping Jen from the circuit.

Jen trudged closer, her eyes heavy. A knot of unease formed in Colt's chest. It looked as though she'd got as little sleep as he had. If he had to guess, he'd say Margaret's snoring had probably been just as loud in the guest room as it had been in the truck during the journey here.

He longed to reach out and tug Jen close. Slide his hands over her back and press his lips to her silky hair. But that would only increase his desire to do more, which would threaten the fragile rebuilding of their friendship and steal his focus from Margaret.

"How about we just walk him around a bit?" Jen suggested, drawing Diamond to a halt in front of Margaret. "Let him explore the ranch?" She smiled. "You could help hold his lead."

Margaret watched the big animal for a moment, then bent over and brushed a speck of mud off the toe of her shoe. Just as she had several times throughout the day when she'd declined an offer with silence.

Muffled groans broke out behind them.

"We got other horses," Kayden said, trailing a hand slowly along the top rung of the fence he and Jayden sat on. "Some of 'em ain't as big as Diamond. And they're slower."

Jayden puffed a gnat out of the corner of his mouth. "Yeah. We got ponies, too." He looked down, frowning and swinging his feet. "They're a lot slower."

Colt smiled at the world-weary note in Jayden's tone. It was clear Dominic had persuaded the boys to spend the day showing Margaret around. They'd issued the invitation first thing that morning, before gobbling down their breakfast. Then they had bounced their knees impatiently as they'd waited for Margaret to finish picking at her food so they could get started.

Unfortunately, that was how the boys had spent the entire day—issuing invitations in hopes that Margaret would respond favorably. But she never did. She'd just hung back and stepped carefully along the winding paths of the ranch as they'd toured.

"I don't mean to be a bad sport or nothin', Mr. Colt," Jayden said, squinting up at him. "But today's almost gone and we ain't really done nothing yet. We don't got long, you know? Spring break won't last for forever."

"Yeah." Kayden untucked his feet from the lower fence rail and jumped to the ground. "School starts back up next week and we had every day planned out. We were gonna build a fort today, shoot the BB guns tomorrow, go to a pool party on Wednesday..."

Colt stilled as Kayden rambled on. One week. That's all he had. And he'd wasted a whole day with no progress to show for it, feeling even more removed from his little sister than before they arrived.

He closed his eyes, frustration making

his muscles seize. *Strike two for lousy big brother.*

"We already got a bunch of wood for the fort," Kayden said, jumping over a deep mud hole behind Margaret and stepping to her side. "It's stacked up by the shed and Uncle Dominic said we could use as much as we wanted." His expression turned hopeful. "Wanna help us build the fort instead, Margaret? You ain't got to ride a horse if you're too scared."

Her head shot up. "I'm not scared."

Kayden smirked. "Yeah, right."

Colt cast his eyes heavenward. Perfect. The last thing they needed today was a mini showdown.

"All right, that's enough," he said. "Margaret's not scared. She just doesn't feel like riding a horse right now. That's all."

Kayden shrugged. "If you say so. But being scared ain't no big deal. She's a girl."

Margaret scowled. "So?"

"So—" Kayden splayed his hands "—girls are always scared of somethin'."

"No, we're not," she snapped.

"Let's forget about riding for now," Jen said, leading her horse forward a few steps. "Why don't I untack Diamond and then we can go in for a while and get a soda or something?"

*"Go in?"* Jayden cried. He climbed down from the fence and darted over. "You mean we don't get to do nothing fun today?"

An ache formed behind Colt's eyes. He rubbed his temple and glanced at Jen's dismayed expression. Her thoughts were clear in the lines of strain on her face—the same thoughts he was sifting through at that exact moment.

How in the world did someone go about appeasing three disagreeable kids? And why had he put Jen and himself in the position of having to do it?

"Yep," Kayden grumbled. "We gotta go in because Margaret's too scared to do anything."

"I'm not scared," she retorted.

"Yeah, you are. 'Cause you're a girl. All girls are scared."

Colt held up a hand. "Kids—"

"That's not true." Margaret balled her hands into fists. "You're just ignorant."

"No, I ain't." Kayden flushed, glancing at his brother and whispering, "What's ignorant mean?"

Jayden shrugged. "I don't know."

"No one's scared *or* ignorant." Colt blew out a breath and headed for the gate. "And we're going in."

"I'll ride him."

Colt stopped and glanced over his shoulder. Margaret dragged her hands over her skirt and took an unsteady step toward Diamond.

Unease trickled down Colt's spine as he eyed her awkward posture. "I don't think it's a good idea right now, Margaret. You don't have to ride if you don't feel like it. We can always try again tomorrow."

"No," she said. "I want to ride today."

Her voice shook, but she took another hesitant step. Sensing her movement, Diamond tilted his ears in her direction and jerked his broad head toward her.

The girl started, then stumbled backward over the uneven ground and plopped into the mud behind her with a splash.

"Oh, no," Jen gasped, releasing Diamond's reins and rushing over.

Colt reached the girl first, crouched at her side and helped her sit up with a hand on her elbow.

Margaret looked down at her soaked clothes and submerged feet. Her shoulders jerked as she broke into loud sobs, and she covered her face with muddy hands.

Colt patted her shoulder awkwardly, eyeing her small frame and asking, "Are you hurt?"

Her sobs grew louder. He glanced up, meeting Jen's worried gaze. She looked as lost as he felt.

"Hey," Kayden said, kneeling at Margaret's side and touching her shoulder. "I didn't mean what I said. And we ain't got to ride the horses. We can go in if you want."

Margaret bent over farther and pulled her knees to her chest, her breathing turning hoarse.

"It's all right, now," Colt soothed, rubbing a hand over her back. "Everything's okay. Everyone has a bad spill now and then. We'll go inside and get you cleaned up."

She curled into a tighter ball, rocking slightly.

Colt's chest ached. "Everything's okay—"

"N-no, it's n-not," she cried, struggling for air. "N-nothing's okay."

Margaret raised her head and shoved hard at Colt's shoulders. He rocked back on his heels, bracing himself on the ground as she scrambled to her feet.

The girl's hair tumbled in slimy clumps

around her red face, and her muddied skirt clung to her legs. She bent over and rubbed furiously at the sludge covering her shoes. The formerly pink sneakers were covered in thick brown mud. Not a speck of the bright color remained.

Her face crumpled. "They're r-ruined."

"I'll get you new ones," Colt said hastily, standing. "First thing tomorrow."

She shook her head and squeezed her eyes shut. "My m-mother gave me these."

Colt winced, his throat closing. He reached for her. "I'm sorry, Marg—"

"No." She sidestepped him, shaking violently and backing away. "I don't want you. I want… I want…"

Her gaze flicked from him and Jen to the boys, tears coursing down her cheeks. Another sob escaped her and she spun away, ducking between the fence rails and running toward the house.

"I didn't mean to make her cry again," Kayden said quietly, studying the ground. "I'm sorry, Mr. Colt. I really am."

Colt swallowed the lump in his throat and lowered his head, avoiding Jen's eyes. He was sorry, too. Sorry he'd left the circuit and put Jen in this position. Sorry he was arrogant enough to believe he could ever play at being a decent brother. And sorry as hell he'd dragged Margaret away from the only home she'd ever known, to surround her with strangers. Because that was exactly what he was to her. A stranger.

*I don't want you.*

Colt walked away, taking swift strides toward the bunkhouse. *Strike three.* This was the biggest mistake he'd ever made.

# Chapter 6

Jen hesitated, shifting from one foot to the other in the hallway, then raised her fist and knocked on the bedroom door.

"Margaret?"

No response. Not that she'd expected one. Jen pressed her ear to the wood and strained to catch any sounds from the other side. Margaret's cries had finally subsided and only a few sniffs were audible now.

After the unpleasant scene a few minutes earlier, Colt and Margaret had taken off in opposite directions. It'd been difficult to choose which one to pursue first. The defeated slump of Colt's shoulders had intensified the ache in

Jen's chest just as much as Margaret's stumbling steps had. And she'd longed to comfort Colt.

But Margaret's choked sobs had won out, leading Jen to leave Diamond with a ranch hand so she could make her way up to the main house. Hopefully, easing Margaret's pain would help relieve Colt's, too.

"Margaret? I'm coming in, okay?"

Jen turned the door handle and entered quietly. She blinked as her eyes adjusted to the darkness of the room, then focused on the small lump in the center of one of the twin beds. Margaret rolled to the side and hugged her knees to her chest, the sheet wrinkling beneath her muddy legs.

"Do you mind if I open the window?" Jen asked, crossing the room. "It's a bit stuffy in here."

Margaret flopped over and buried her face in the pillow.

Jen frowned. Seemed like every Mead she met was intent upon turning their back to her. The action was yet another similarity Margaret shared with Colt. They both pushed people away.

Jen swept the curtain back and lifted the window, inhaling the surge of fresh air. She stood in the stream of sunlight, lingering over the scent of honeysuckle and pine, and searching for the right approach.

What could she possibly say to a child who'd just lost both parents? And was there any use for words at all under these circumstances?

She couldn't remember how she'd been soothed as a child after losing her father. He'd died when she was five, but she'd been too young to really understand what she'd lost. Or remember him now.

His name had disappeared over the years, Jen's mother the only one remembering or saying it. Apparently, a small-town mechanic with greasy hands and few customers didn't stick in folks' memories too well.

Jen walked over and hovered by the bed. "May I sit down for a minute?"

Margaret's grubby fingers pulled the edges of the pillow tighter over her face.

Grimacing at the muddy footprints on the hardwood floor, Jen sat. "I've made a mess." She lifted her right leg and tugged at her wet boot. "If there's dirt in a ten-mile radius, my boots will attract it." She shrugged. "Well, in this case, mud."

Still no response.

"Good thing I've had lots of experience with it," she continued, pulling her foot free and laughing. "I'm a pretty messy girl, you know? So I always pack an extra pair and I've learned exactly what to do to get them looking good as new again."

The bed shifted. Jen looked over her shoulder to find Margaret's brown eyes peeking above the white pillow.

"Goo'…a'…'ew?" Margaret asked, her words muffled by the pillow.

"Yep." Jen proceeded to remove her other boot. "A day as warm and sunny as this, all you have to do is set them out on the front porch and let them bake until they dry. Then bang 'em until all the dried clumps fall off."

Margaret lifted her face, her muddy hair plastered to her flushed cheeks. "Does it work with sneakers?"

Jen pursed her lips. "Mostly. Sometimes they look a bit worse for wear, but that just gives them character."

Margaret glanced down and picked at a dried glob of mud on her knee. "Could you do mine, too?"

"Sure," Jen said, inspecting the girl's damaged shoes. "Might need to scrub them with a toothbrush afterward, but I think there's a good chance I'll get most of that pretty pink back."

Margaret sat up and wiped her eyes. "I could help."

"I'd appreciate that," Jen said. "Sometimes I have trouble getting the laces good and clean, but I expect if we worked together, we could handle it. And I got to thinking…" She hesitated, then reached out and rubbed a smudge of mud from Margaret's cheek with her thumb. "There's a lot more dirt, bugs and horse patties out here than you're used to. So it might be a good idea for us to go shopping tomorrow. Get you a pair of jeans and some boots, maybe?"

"Okay." Margaret sniffed, her brow wrinkling. "But what's a horse patty?"

"The same thing as a cow patty except it comes from horses." Jen grinned. "Poop."

The girl laughed. A real honest-to-goodness giggle that brightened her face. The gleam in her eyes and tilt of her mouth were so similar to Colt's.

Jen caught her breath at the sight, an affection she always felt looking at Colt welling inside her.

Margaret began untying the laces on one shoe and Jen tackled the other, trying not to show the sappy feelings coursing through her. Jen would be leaving soon and the less attached Margaret became to her, the better.

"Hi, guys," a voice called from the doorway. "Hope we're not interrupting."

A short, blonde woman stood in the doorway with a pair of black-haired twin toddlers at her side.

"No, not at all," Jen said, smiling. "Margaret, this is Cissy, Dominic's wife. You turned in so early last night, I don't think you had a chance to meet her."

"Hello," Margaret said, eyes lingering on the little girls.

"It's nice to meet you, Margaret. I'm sorry we didn't get to talk at breakfast this morning." Cissy gestured at the twin girls as they waddled toward the bed. "These two were cranky and didn't want to cooperate, so we didn't make it down in time." She laughed and glanced at Jen. "Can I still blame it on the terrible twos if they're not quite two yet?"

"Aw, they get a free pass for being so cute," Jen teased, bending down to kiss one twin's smooth cheek as the toddler hugged her leg. The girls' raven hair and blue eyes were identical, making it impossible to tell them apart. "Who do I have here?"

"Gwen," Cissy said with pride, before pointing to the other toddler. "That's Grace."

Grace grabbed the sheet and pulled, scrambling onto the bed. She stood by Margaret, examined her bedraggled hair, then touched it.

"Ew," Grace said, shifting her attention to Margaret's face.

Margaret squeezed her eyes shut as the child's grasping fingers traveled over her nose and mouth. Grace gurgled, patted Margaret's cheeks, then plopped onto her lap, evoking another laugh from Margaret.

"I think Grace has claimed you as a new friend, Margaret," Cissy said, smiling. "Kayden has, too. He asked me to check on you. Tell you he was sorry for what happened."

Margaret shook her head, watching as Grace's small fingers picked at her muddy skirt. "It wasn't Kayden's fault." She glanced at Jen. "I…guess I was afraid of Diamond."

Jen squeezed the girl's knee. "A lot of people are nervous around horses. I can help you get to know him better, if you'd like."

Margaret nodded and reached down to steady Grace, who bounced excitedly in her lap.

"I was just about to take the girls down to

the creek," Cissy said. "We have about an hour to explore before it gets dark. Would you like to join us, Margaret? We could help you wash that mud off, and then come in, grab a bite to eat and watch a movie afterward."

Margaret flashed an excited smile at Jen. "May I go with them?"

"Sure," Jen said. "Have fun. I'll put our shoes out in the sun, then tomorrow morning we can get started cleaning them."

A quick thank-you and Margaret left with Cissy, giggling again as a twin grabbed each of her hands and wobbled along at her sides.

Jen's shoulders relaxed on a rush of warmth. A child's laugh had never sounded so sweet.

After setting the muddy footwear on the porch steps, Jen put on a clean pair of boots and made her way around to the nearest guest wing. She heard the thump and creak of a truck bed being loaded as she rounded the corner. Colt's pickup was parked in front of the open door, tailgate down.

Moments later, Colt appeared, hauling a covered bucket. He halted at the sight of her, then ducked his head and eased past her, sliding the bucket onto the truck bed between two others with more focus than necessary.

Jen tensed. "What are you doing?"

"Storing water for Diamond." He spun and walked away, saying over his shoulder as he entered the guest room, "He didn't take to the taste in Longview last year."

Longview? Jen stilled. Texas. He was packing for Texas.

She followed him inside and closed the door.

Colt stood in front of the dresser, pulling out drawers, scooping up the contents and dumping them into his overnight bag.

"If we leave first thing tomorrow, we can both make the next competition without having to break our necks to get there." He emptied another drawer. "I called Tammy. She's booking us some rooms at that same motel we stayed in last year. Cheap but decent."

Jen eyed the set of his shoulders and his jerky movements. She was so tempted to agree. To throw her own things in a bag and spend the next hour planning out the fastest route to Longview.

But Margaret's mud-slicked sneakers were busy baking under the sun. And Margaret was probably at the creek right now, splashing in the water with Cissy's girls, laughing and soothing herself with the knowledge that her shoes might regain some life tomorrow with Jen's help.

The wave of guilt sweeping through Jen overpowered her longing to abandon the plan and return to the circuit immediately. She couldn't break her word to Margaret or encourage Colt to do the same.

"Have you thought this through, Colt?" she asked.

His T-shirt strained over the thick muscles of his back as he lifted his overnight bag, then dropped it on top of the dresser. "We have to leave soon if we want to make the first round."

"What about Margaret?"

He slammed the middle drawer shut with his knee. "We swing through Atlanta, drop her off, then take a shortcut to the interstate. Won't lose but a few hours."

"Is that all?" Jen asked softly. "I think you stand to lose a lot more than that."

His broad hands stilled over the bag.

"I know I was against this," she said. "No one hates leaving the circuit more than I do, and if this is really what you want then I'm all for it. But I think you were right about Margaret needing a break."

"This was a mistake," he said. "It's not working."

"We've barely started and we've never been quitters. If we were to give up now, I'd think you'd regret it before we crossed the state line."

Colt shook his head. "I was foolish to think I could pull this off. She's doing worse here than she was there. You saw her earlier."

"Yeah. I did. I saw her have a healthy cry. One I suspect was long overdue. You're not alone in this, Colt. I'm with you. Dom and Cissy are with you. We're all ready and willing to help. But this won't work if you don't open up." Jen moved close, placing a hand on his back. "I think it'd be good for you to take some time for yourself, too. Take time to grieve—"

"I don't know what you want from me, Jen," he bit out, yanking the zipper shut on the bag.

"Just talk to me," she said. "Tell me what you're feeling."

"I don't feel anything." He shrugged off her touch, strode across the room and slumped on the edge of the bed.

"You just lost your father," she whispered. "I know you feel something—"

"I don't feel a damn thing, because I barely knew him. Is that what you want to hear?" He balled his fists on his knees, the knuckles turning white. "He was never around and the times he did show up, all he did was criticize or judge. Margaret and I were no more than possessions to him. Something to show off at parties. A way to pass himself off as a family man." Colt refused to look at her, staring over her left shoulder. "He was a cold, heartless bastard and I hated hi—"

His voice broke, a ragged breath lifting his chest. He dropped his head into his hands and his shoulders jerked.

Jen sat at his side and pulled him close. She smoothed her fingers through his blond hair and tugged gently at the back of his neck, bringing his face to her chest and cradling him. His strong arms slipped around her waist, squeezing so hard the painful grip stole the air from her lungs. But she held on.

"I'm sorry, Colt," she whispered, rocking him gently back and forth. "So sorry."

He didn't make a sound, but his body shook and he slid his face down, burying it against her belly. Her shirt grew damp under his cheek, her heart beating harder with every silent heave of his shoulders and renewed bout of moist warmth soaking into her middle. She paused every few minutes to wipe away tears of her own and held back as many as she could.

Finally, his hold on her loosened and he raised his head. He opened his mouth but hesitated, no sound emerging.

The bereft expression crossing his striking features stabbed her chest. She leaned in, dropping soft kisses over his forehead, cheeks and bearded jaw, hoping to lessen the heavy shadows hanging over him.

He looked at her then, his blue eyes welling, tears clinging to the ends of his thick lashes. She pressed gentle kisses there, too. The taste of salt touched her tongue as his eyelids fluttered shut.

His strong hand slid into her hair, palm cupping the back of her head and fingers kneading her nape. "Jen?"

The husky whisper had barely escaped when he touched his mouth to hers.

Her belly fluttered at the light, coaxing movements of his lips. A gentle throb began in her belly, then moved through her blood, clouding her thoughts but heightening her senses. His masculine scent enveloped her, and each stroke of his callused fingers against her skin sent more thrills through her body.

Colt drew back with heavy breaths, his gaze lingering on her mouth and a plea lighting his eyes. Grief hung thickly around them, removing logic and obscuring good intentions.

Trembling, Jen rested her palms against the hard wall of his chest. She should say no and sidestep regret before it had a chance to edge between them. Let him go; stand up and leave him to grieve in private.

But her body ached to comfort him. And her heart strained to absorb his pain.

She moved closer, sliding her arms around his back and parting his lips with hers. "Yes."

Colt opened his eyes and blinked, adjusting to the darkness surrounding him. A weak ray of light pierced the dark interior of the room. Gentle air whispered over his bare chest and he glanced down, breath catching at the fiery spill of red hair across his skin.

*Jen.* He closed his eyes. God forgive him.

His hands tightened around her, the graceful curves of her shoulder and hip filling his palms. The tips of his fingers tingled from the silky feel of her skin. Just as they had hours earlier when he'd unhooked her bra, then smoothed gentle circles over her back. When he'd unbuttoned her jeans and slid them down her legs, his mouth tracing her toned thighs.

He gritted his teeth, attempting to tamp down the enticing thoughts. Even now, his tongue drifted over his bottom lip, seeking one more sweet taste of her kiss. Wanting to hold on to her as long as possible.

His heart tripped in his chest, the jolt sending a chill through him. He shouldn't have done it. Shouldn't have kissed her or taken comfort in her sweet warmth. But her gentle touch had filled the dark hollow in his gut and brightened his gloom. And when her body had wrapped as tightly around him as her soothing whisper, he'd surrendered completely. He'd focused solely on the pleasurable throb in his blood and her welcoming embrace.

Colt held his breath and moved carefully, easing Jen onto the pillow as he slid from beneath her. A quiet murmur escaped her and she shifted into a more comfortable position, settling back to sleep.

Colt sat up on the thick mattress and dropped his bare feet to the hardwood floor. He rubbed his palms over his thighs, savoring the last hum of sleep pulsing through him, reluctant to leave Jen's side. But he forced himself to pad over to the window.

He pushed the curtains back and cracked opened the window to discover a chorus of croaks and chirps drifting on the warm breeze. The sun had almost set and dusk was falling. He and Jen had spent a little over an hour in bed.

He hooked his fingers on top of the window frame, dropped his head and leaned forward, stretching the muscles of his shoulders and neck. Sighing, he raised back up and surveyed the moonlit ranch outside.

Raintree's grounds were peaceful, the riding trails, pond and wide, grassy fields empty. He could just make out the low lights escaping from the stables down the hill. The hands' silhouettes moved in and out of it, performing the evening duties, their laughter ringing in the night air.

He smiled. Raintree was more beautiful than he remembered. Every corner of it was full of laughter and comforts, the kind of supportive and rejuvenating surroundings he'd hoped would help Meg...

*Margaret.* He squeezed his eyes shut, gut churning.

At the quiet rustle of sheets, he glanced

over his shoulder. Jen's knees drew up toward her chest, her red curls dancing over her back with the push of the breeze.

Colt crossed the room and reached for the blanket, tugging it up from the foot of the bed and drawing it over her. His eyes followed the trail of beard-burn marks scattered over her pale thighs, hips and breasts, her bare limbs shivering as he covered them.

*That hurts.*

Margaret's words from days ago returned. Colt shook his head and rubbed a hand over his face, his palm rasping against his beard. Margaret had refused his offer of comfort so abruptly that he wondered if she'd ever been hugged.

He cringed. Knowing his cold father, she probably hadn't. But their father had taught Margaret other things. She'd learned to remain detached and unfeeling to the point of not being able to stand anyone's touch. Least of all Colt's. Because in her eyes, he was an absent and uncaring son of a bitch like their father. And up to this point, he had been.

Still was, in fact. He should never have considered leaving Raintree after the first setback. And he should've been with Margaret for the past hour instead of lying in bed seeking comfort with Jen.

Colt sat beside Jen and brushed a strand of hair from her face. His hand stilled, a realization hitting him hard in the gut.

He'd never returned to the same bed after leaving a woman in it. Had always grabbed his things and left, never looking back or seeking anything permanent. But none of those women had been Jen, and he found himself wanting to stay. Wanting to sink right back into the mattress, gather her against his chest and cling to the comforting warmth he'd discovered in her arms a few hours ago.

Only, that would mean putting his own interests before Margaret's. An act that would make him no better than his father—a man who had chosen his career and a succession of wives over his children.

Careful not to wake her, he brushed a kiss across Jen's brow, then tucked the cover more securely around her shoulders. He grabbed his bag and edged into the small bathroom.

Flicking on the fluorescent light above the sink, he winced at the bright glare and studied his face in the mirror. It was so similar to John W. Mead's. The same eyes and nose. A Mead man through and through. The kind of man who never stuck around and always took the easy way out. One who would ship Margaret off to boarding school for most of her life. One who would pack his bags, load his truck and take off, leaving Margaret behind without a second thought.

*You're more like your father than you think.*

Colt raked his nails through his beard, the phrase cutting through him. He'd done everything possible to rebel against his father. Had left home for the circuit, refused to take part in his father's business and grown a beard to hide the features that looked so similar to a man he no longer respected. And by doing so, he'd become no better than his father.

Colt straightened. It was time to stop running. He may look like John W. Mead but he was a different man. A better one. A man who would live up to his responsibilities and put his family first.

He dug his shaving kit out, retrieved a razor and got started.

Ten minutes later, he tossed the dull blade in the trash and unstopped the sink, running a hand over his clean-shaven jaw as the dirty water gurgled away.

"Colt?"

He heard the bed creak, then shuffling movements and the light click on.

Heart stalling, he dressed quickly then stepped out of the bathroom.

"Colt—" Jen jerked to a stop in the middle of the room, her hesitant smile slowly melting away as she paused in the act of buttoning her jeans.

His face heated and he swept a hand over his cheek. "You don't like it."

She blinked and shook her head, her shiny hair spilling over her shoulders. "No. I mean, yeah. I do." She adjusted the collar of her T-shirt and cleared her throat. "I like it. It's just… different."

*Different.* Colt blew out a rough breath. Different like the strength of the feelings coursing through him. Feelings he'd always had for Jen but ones which had intensified.

"I'm sorry, Jen." Colt cringed at the strained sound of his voice, his hands spreading helplessly in front of him. "I didn't mean for things to go as far as they did."

"It's okay," she said quietly. "I wanted to. It was…" Her face flushed and a small smile emerged. "I enjoyed it."

So had he. And if circumstances were different, her tender grin would be a welcome relief.

The hopeful expression on Jen's face made his chest clench painfully at what he had to do. Colt looked away, focusing on the flutter of the curtains over the window and digging deep for the right words.

"I think you were right about staying," he said. "I'd like to give things with Margaret another try and I could still use your help." He sucked in a strong breath. "I want you, Jen. But I need to concentrate on rebuilding a relationship with Margaret and I think it's best if my attention is on her right now. What we just did doesn't have to change anything between us," he stressed, trying to convince himself as much as her. "We can pretend it didn't happen. Forget…"

*Forget the sweet taste of her skin against his tongue. Like warm honey. The soft press of her breasts against his chest. Like—*

"We can forget it happened," he choked out, facing her. "Go back to the way things were."

Jen's expression dimmed and her smile vanished. "Yeah." She ducked her head and moved toward the door, her long hair obscuring her face and muffling her words. "That's probably for the best."

"Red?" Colt forced himself to root his boots to the floor and ball his hands into fists to prevent himself from reaching for her. He could endure her disappointment in him but not the thought of her feeling betrayed by him. "Nothing happened between me and Autumn. I left that bar with her, but that's as far as it went. And that's the God's honest truth."

Jen's hand stilled on the doorknob and her back stiffened. She stayed silent for a few moments, then asked, "Why tell me this now?"

"Because I know what you're thinking." His throat tightened and it hurt to speak. "And I won't be that guy anymore, you know? Not with you."

She looked over her shoulder, her features clouded with confusion.

"Your friendship means more to me than any fling ever could." He shook his head. "I won't risk losing that. I won't treat you the way I treated other women."

Her features cleared and her eyes turned sad. "But despite all of your good intentions, isn't that exactly what you're doing now? Pushing me away? Reminding me of my place?"

His lungs constricted, making it hard to drag in a breath. "No. That's not—"

"Let's forget about it, Colt. Just like you

said." She sighed heavily. "It's getting late. Margaret's probably looking for us. I told her I'd take her shopping tomorrow, and you've got enough to deal with right now." Her face flushed, her tone hardening. "Besides, it's my fault. I knew the score going in."

Colt stood still after she left, listening as the spring chorus of night life filled the room, and waited for the familiar relief to set in. The kind he'd felt after every other sexual encounter had ended. The one he experienced when he was alone again. Free of obligation to a woman.

But it never came. And the hours he spent tossing and turning that night proved the emptiness on the other side of the bed had crept its way into his heart.

## Chapter 7

Jen bent, slipped the jeans under the dressing room door and wiggled them. "These are the last two styles in your size, Margaret. How are the shirts working out? Do you need me to grab you a few more?"

"No, thank you." A small hand shot out and tugged the jeans into the dressing room. "I think I found some I like."

Jen's shoulders sagged and she smiled. *Thank goodness.*

It'd taken an hour to make the drive from Raintree to Trudy's Treasures, which, according to Cissy, was the best clothing store near the ranch. It'd taken another hour for

Margaret to browse the entire clothing section and the past hour for her to try on every garment within her size range. And this had all begun at nine o'clock this morning, after they'd spent the first two hours of daylight banging the mud off Margaret's sneakers and scrubbing them with a toothbrush until they were pink again.

Jen straightened and puffed a strand of hair out of her face, trying to keep the relief in her voice to a minimum. "Good. Come out and show me whenever you're ready, okay?"

"Okay," Margaret said.

The clang of hangers and rustle of clothing resumed on the other side of the door. Jen started for the chairs in the waiting area, a restless sensation buzzing down her legs. The nagging thought that she needed to get back to the ranch and spend some time with Diamond returned. It had been four days now since she'd left the circuit. She hadn't checked her stats or squeezed in a lick of training yet.

But Jen was surprised to discover the anxiety she usually felt about not practicing had diminished. That each hour she'd spent with Margaret—though exhausting—had relaxed her nerves.

"Just look at what I found!" Trudy, a pretty

brunette with teased hair and big earrings, held up two cowgirl hats. "They'd go perfect with that beautiful blond hair of hers."

Jen shook her head. Hats? That'd add another hour to their shopping visit and delay her training even more. "Oh no, please—"

"Don't worry," Trudy said with a laugh. "Given the pile of clothes she's already put by the register, I can stand to throw in a couple hats for free." She looked over her shoulder and grinned, voice lowering to a whisper. "I think your husband's getting a bit restless."

Jen leaned to the side and peered past her. Colt shifted in his chair across the room, closing his eyes and leaning his head back against the window. Jen's fingers tingled, wanting to rove over the strong line of his freshly shaved jaw and trace the contours of his muscular chest. She wanted to wrap her arms around him just as she had last night.

Only, she knew exactly where that would lead.

Jen ignored the heat scorching her cheeks. "He's not my husband."

"Oh?" Trudy's pink mouth stayed suspended in a perfect oval for a moment, her perfectly manicured eyebrows lifting. "Boyfriend, then?"

Jen shook her head. "We're just friends."

*Just friends*, she repeated silently. That was all. Last night was a onetime thing. A moment of weakness for them both that would never happen again.

*I want you, Jen. But I need to concentrate on rebuilding a relationship with Margaret...*

She looked down and shoved her hands in her pockets, the pain in her chest strengthening. Colt had chosen to do the honorable thing and focus on supporting his sister. Something she'd promised to do as well.

Jen repeated her words with conviction. "We're friends. That's all."

Trudy giggled and leaned in, whispering, "Well, he sure is a handsome devil."

"Yeah." She forced a grin. That was something she couldn't argue with.

The shopkeeper's smile widened. "I'll just slip these to our VIP and see how she's doing."

Trudy swept off toward the dressing room, the aroma of hair spray and floral perfume trailing in her wake.

Jen rubbed her brow and headed for an empty chair, avoiding Colt's narrowed eyes as she sat next to him. He'd studied her with the same expression almost a dozen times across the breakfast table this morning and at least once every mile during the drive into town.

"You all right?" he asked, leaning forward and propping his elbows on his knees.

He'd rolled his sleeves up and the defined muscles of his forearms were on full display as he dangled his hands between his legs. Hands that had caressed every part of her last night. Skilled fingers that had—

"Yeah." Jen cleared her throat, trying not to savor his spicy, male scent. "I'm fine."

He dipped his blond head in the direction of the dressing room. "Margaret getting close to finishing up?"

Jen nodded. "I think she's on the last round. We should be able to head out soon."

"Thank God for that." Colt chuckled. "I've never spent this much time shopping in my entire life."

A fresh surge of longing coursed through Jen at the deep tone of his laugh and wide smile.

She stifled a groan of frustration. He'd shaved. So what? The look wasn't *that* different. His eyes were still the same crystal blue she'd admired countless times in the past—without this strong a reaction. His features were still as handsome as they'd always been—no surprise there.

"I told you this morning that you didn't need to drive us," she said. "Cissy gave me good directions and I'd have found the place okay."

"I know." His mouth wobbled slightly, the smile slipping from the sensual curves. "I wanted to come. Wanted to spend time with Margaret." His voice lowered, his lips barely moving as he continued, "And with you."

Jen stilled. That was what it was. She'd never had a clear view of his lips before. And now she knew exactly how they felt when he—

She tore her eyes from his face and focused on the floor, hoping he didn't notice the heat snaking down her neck at the last three words he'd said.

"Jen." Colt shifted, his tanned hand landing gently on her thigh. "I..."

The heat of his palm seeped through the denim of her jeans and trailed up her leg to pool in her belly. She tensed then pulled away, fighting the urge to lean into him.

He muttered a curse, withdrawing his hand and shuffling his boots awkwardly across the floor.

Jen gritted her teeth and stared at the dressing room door. Colt had touched her out of habit, just as he had a thousand times over the past several years. She was sure of it. And she wouldn't look for something more. Something a friend wouldn't notice or anticipate. And something she was ashamed to admit she still craved despite their agreement to forget.

Jen closed her eyes and blew out a breath. What a great friend she was. Lusting after a grieving man. Wanting things he would never have agreed to last night had she not pushed.

It was time to set this longing for Colt down. Put it behind her and get back to the business of racing—the one thing she should be focused on above all others. The success she'd worked so hard for was too precious to let slip away because of one night of weakness.

"We need to talk," he said in a low rasp. "I know I said we should put last night behind us but—"

"How's this look?"

The dressing room door squeaked on its hinges as Margaret emerged, strutting to a stop in front of them.

Grateful for the distraction, Jen scooted to

the edge of her chair and waved a hand. "Turn around so I can get the full effect."

Margaret did, then propped her hands on her hips and tipped her head back, her blond curls bouncing under her tan cowgirl hat. The blue button-down shirt she wore matched her eyes and the jeans fit perfectly with the aid of a wide belt.

"Ms. Trudy said it's authentic Western wear and that it's just right for staying on a ranch," Margaret said. She touched her jeans pocket. "There are rhinestones just like yours, Ms. Jen." She pointed a toe and turned her foot from side to side. "And the boots have pink stitching, too."

Jen laughed, unexpected pleasure bubbling in her belly and easing her discomfort. "They certainly do."

She had to hand it to Trudy. The brown boots with pink accents suited Margaret perfectly. As did the rest of the ensemble. And the proud tilt of Margaret's chin made every hour of scrubbing shoes and scouring Trudy's clothing aisles worth it.

"I love it," Jen added.

Margaret bit her lip and sneaked a glance at her brother from beneath the brim of her hat. "What do you think?"

Colt stood, his gaze moving from Margaret to Jen and then back as he said, "I think you look beautiful. Like a real cowgirl."

Margaret's smile almost blinded them both.

It took an additional twenty minutes to pay for the mountain of clothes and haul them to Colt's truck.

"I'm hungry," Margaret said, skipping to the tailgate and pointing at a diner across the road. "Can we eat there before we go back to the ranch? Ms. Trudy said they have the best hash browns on the planet."

"Well, Ms. Trudy hasn't been wrong yet, has she?" Colt asked, taking his sister's elbow and halting her eager steps as a truck swept past them. He held out his other hand. "How 'bout it, Red?"

*He sure is a handsome devil.* Jen's belly warmed.

Margaret smiled and threw out her hand, too. "Come on, Ms. Jen."

Jen hesitated for a moment, eyes roving over the two siblings. They were a striking pair. Colt, tall and muscular, holding his sister's arm protectively. And Margaret, her eyes bright and welcoming.

The sight of them stirred a strong rush of feeling in Jen's chest, but she tamped it down, forcing herself to focus on the training that needed to be undertaken when she returned to the ranch. And it wouldn't hurt to eat a good lunch before she started.

She edged past Colt's outstretched arm and slipped her hand around Margaret's. She felt the weight of Colt's scrutiny more than once as they crossed the street, the girl bouncing between them excitedly. They made their way into the diner and settled in a corner booth.

"There's so much to choose from," Margaret said, eyes flicking over the menu and knees bouncing under the table.

"Order whatever you'd like. If you're in the mood for a peanut butter and honey sandwich, we can ask if they'll make you one." Colt stretched his brawny arm across the top of the seat above his sister's head. "Though I'm sure it won't be as good as Jen's."

His gaze settled on her, his gentle expression warming Jen's cheeks. She grabbed her water and shuddered at how cold it was.

"I'd like to try the hash browns," Margaret said. "But they have grilled cheese sandwiches, too." She leaned forward, brow furrowing as she read the menu. "And they've got a chee-paht-el…"

"Chipotle," Colt corrected, grinning.

"Chipotle," Margaret repeated. "A chipotle burger. That sounds good, too."

"Chipotles are kind of hot," Jen said. "It might be a little too spicy for you."

The excited gleam in Margaret's eyes dulled slightly.

"I tell you what," Colt said, collecting the menus and tapping them into a stack on the table. "How about we order all three and share? That way you can get a taste of everything."

Margaret perked up. "Can we get chocolate milk shakes, too?"

Colt laughed. "Chocolate milk shakes, too."

The diner was a bit run-down but the service was top-notch. An older woman with graying hair and a wrinkled smile waited on them and took an instant liking to Margaret. She returned to the booth several times to top Margaret's milk shake off with a fresh squirt of whipped cream and regale them with more anecdotes about her grandchildren.

The waitress had just left them laughing over her most recent tale of Budd Jr. when the timer on Colt's wristwatch beeped.

"Switch," he said.

Jen dropped her fork, shoved her plate of hash browns toward Colt, then caught the grilled cheese platter spinning across the table from Margaret's direction.

Margaret laughed. "You almost weren't fast enough that time, Ms. Jen."

"Oh, I'm always fast," she said, winking. "But I'll be faster once I get back to training. Which is something I need to start on as soon as we get back to Raintree."

"For the rodeo, right?" Margaret asked. "Mrs. Cissy told me you and Diamond barrel race."

"Yep. And it won't be long before I compete again."

Jen's hands began to shake. She eyed them closely and tried to still the tremors.

Catching Colt's gaze on her, she gestured toward the ketchup on her fingers. "Will you hand me a napkin, please?"

Colt tugged one from the dispenser and pressed it into her palm. He frowned as he examined her face, and his fingertips hovered against her skin longer than necessary.

"Bet you can't be in the races if you're not fast," Margaret said, popping a fry into her mouth.

"Sure you can." Jen took a bite of the grilled cheese sandwich and ignored the churn in her stomach. "Everyone has to start somewhere.

Other than training, competing is the best way to learn. You just have to be brave enough to try."

Margaret pondered that as she stared at the chipotle burger.

"Jen might be right about that burger," Colt said, reaching for his sister's plate. "Chipotle peppers are kinda hot. You wanna skip this one?"

"No." Margaret brushed his hand away. "I'd like to try it, please."

Margaret picked up the half-eaten burger and took a small bite, chewing slowly. She made a face and reached for her milk shake. Her throat moved with several hard swallows and a tear escaped her eye.

Colt leaned close, an anxious expression crossing his features.

"It's spicy," Margaret said at last, sitting back and smiling. "But I like it."

He chuckled and dug into his hash browns.

"Colt?" Margaret bit her lip, casting hesitant looks at her brother. "If I promise to try harder, would you help me ride one of the horses?"

Colt stilled. "I'd love to."

They shared a smile and Jen's heart turned over in her chest. She looked away and took another bite of her sandwich.

"Will you help, too, Ms. Jen?" Margaret asked, brows lifting. "Please?"

Jen finished chewing and swallowed, thinking of how much she needed to resume training and how little time she had to prepare for the next race. Both great reasons why she should refuse. But they dissipated at the hopeful expression on Margaret's face.

She nodded slowly and conjured up a smile. "Of course."

The pleasure lighting Colt's blue eyes stole Jen's breath and threatened to melt her into a puddle right there in the booth.

The timer went off again and he dropped his fork, shouting, "Switch."

They slid their plates counterclockwise around the table, laughing. Jen took a bite of the chipotle burger and stole a quick glance at Colt. The lines of strain on his face had eased and the sadness that had fallen over him seemed to be lifting.

Her gaze clung to his chiseled jaw as he drank. She followed his broad hand as he lowered the glass to the table, his blunt fingertips drifting lazily through the condensation. The slow movements were so similar to the gentle touches he'd swept across her skin last night.

Colt glanced up and caught her stare, his

blue eyes peering into hers, then lowering to her mouth and lingering.

The heat in his expression intensified Jen's craving to touch him again. The need to feel his mouth trailing down her neck and over her breasts. To welcome the sculpted weight of his body edging between her thighs, pressing her hips into the mattress.

Jen took another bite of the burger and avoided Colt's gaze, the heat of the chipotles nothing compared to the blaze of desire spiraling through her. It was best to put last night behind her. To forget. But Jen was beginning to wonder if she could. Or—even worse—if she really wanted to.

"Horses can smell fear, you know."

Colt tightened the cinch on the saddle, then straightened and glanced over his shoulder. Jayden sat astride a small mare, holding the reins with one hand and fanning away gnats with his hat. The late afternoon sun blazed overhead and sweat and humidity attracted every mosquito and fly within an eighty-mile radius.

"Yep." Kayden nudged his own horse with his heels, walked him across the field to his brother's side and said, "They got a sick sense."

Colt stifled a laugh. "You mean they have a *sixth* sense."

Kayden shrugged. "Whatever." He leaned forward in his saddle, expression solemn. "Now, I ain't trying to start nothing, Mr. Colt. I done learned my lesson. But Jayden's right. You might wanna tell Margaret about that fear thing. You don't want her climbin' up on Destiny and freakin' her out, do you? Destiny's gettin' kinda old. Maybe she can't take a shock like that."

"Nah." Colt smiled and patted the brown mare behind him. "She'll be fine. Dominic said Destiny has seen her share of nervous guests."

"Maybe," Kayden said, eyebrows rising. "But she ain't seen Margaret."

"Hey, Kayden. Look!" Jayden stood up in his stirrups, waving a hand and pointing.

Margaret and Jen ducked between the fence rails and made their way across the pasture. Margaret walked a foot ahead of Jen, chin lifted and shoulders back, her boots stomping with purpose through the grass.

Colt smiled. Seemed like scouting out new clothes and conquering a chipotle burger had improved Margaret's confidence. Well, that and the oohing and aahing Cissy and her twin girls had done when they'd seen Margaret. He'd barely brought the truck to a halt when his sister had hopped out and scrambled up to the front porch to show off her new look. Colt had left to saddle up Destiny before Margaret changed her mind about riding, stumbling upon the roaming boys in the process.

"She's got a hat," Jayden said.

"And boots," Kayden added, narrowing his eyes as she drew closer. "You said she got some jeans, Mr. Colt. You didn't say nothing 'bout her going straight-up cowgirl."

"Easy, boys," Colt said. "I invited you out here to encourage Margaret and give her moral support, not rattle her. You remember how things ended up yesterday."

"Yes, sir," the twins chimed.

Margaret arrived with Jen close behind, slowing as she neared Destiny and the boys. She drew to a halt and the confidence in her expression faded as she examined the horse.

"Hey, Margaret," Kayden said, straightening in his saddle. "I like your gear."

Her brow furrowed as she squinted up at him. "My gear?"

"He means your hat and boots," Jayden said, jerking his chin. "They're cool lookin'."

Margaret's smile reappeared and she hooked her thumbs in the pockets of her jeans. "Thanks."

"We're glad you're gonna ride with us," Kayden said. "But what about you, Ms. Jen? Where's Diamond?"

"He's out roaming in the pasture with his buddies," she said, placing a palm on Margaret's shoulder. "I'm just going to watch today and be on hand to help if Margaret needs me."

Today. No mention of tomorrow.

Colt froze at the unease invading his gut. It was the same feeling that had taken hold of him in the diner earlier, when Jen had mentioned needing to train and return to competition soon. The nervous tension in her expression had unsettled him. And the possibility of her leaving Raintree earlier than they'd planned had made him reach out and touch her, with the urge to keep her at his side.

Jen had been right last night. He'd treated her exactly as he had other women by suggesting they return to the status quo and avoid a more serious relationship. But how could he make a commitment to Jen without sacrificing time that should be devoted to Margaret?

The sun broke free of a stray cloud, lighting up the field with a golden glow. Colt squinted against the glare and traced the graceful fall of Jen's red hair with his eyes, remembering the pleasant glide of it across his chest and the feel of it between his fingertips.

He didn't want to forget last night. Was damned foolish to think he could. He wanted another night. Needed more of her. More of the intense connection they'd shared. More of her soothing touch and tone. And, though he knew he shouldn't, he wanted her to need him, too.

Jen tapped the brim of Margaret's hat, held up a pink helmet and smiled. "Ready to swap out?"

Margaret nodded. They made swift work of removing the cowboy hat and securing the helmet, Margaret inching closer to Jen's side and casting nervous glances at Destiny every few seconds.

"How 'bout we get you two introduced first?" Colt asked.

He took hold of Destiny's reins and led her toward Margaret, stopping a few feet away. Flies followed them and buzzed around the mare's back end, causing her to flick her tail in a wide arc.

Margaret jumped and moved closer to Jen.

Colt released the reins and walked over, lowering to his haunches in front of Margaret. "You sure you want to do this? There are a lot of other things we can do instead."

Margaret glanced over his shoulder at the boys, then back at Destiny. "I—" Her voice broke, a thread of fear straining it, but she continued, "I want to try."

Jen gathered Margaret's long curls in her hands, sweeping them over the girl's shoulders and bending to whisper in her ear, "We'll be right here with you. Colt and I both. We won't let anything happen to you."

A gentle heat lit in Colt's chest as he listened. The word *we* had never sounded so sweet.

"But what if..." Margaret's voice faded and her face paled. "What if Destiny gets scared or something? She might..."

"Destiny's done this a lot," Jen said. "She's calm. And she's trained to be patient."

"But what if I mess up?" Margaret's eyes widened. "What if I can't hold on?"

"Colt will be right there the whole time," Jen said. "He won't let you fall."

"Have you ever fallen?" Margaret blinked up at Jen, breathing quickly.

"Twice." A smile flitted across her lips. "But I was riding recklessly both times and lost my focus. Colt helped keep me safe." She brushed Margaret's bangs back, tucking them under the helmet. "It doesn't happen as often as you might think. And I promise Colt won't let that happen to you."

Colt glanced up at Jen, chest swelling at the patient look in her brown eyes and the gentle reassurance in her touch. She had to be itching to put out barrels, saddle up Diamond and hit the dirt by now. But she'd put her needs on hold for Margaret. And for him.

He tore his gaze away from the sweet freckles sprinkling her cheeks and the cute dimple in her chin, focusing on Margaret's wary frown as it dissolved.

"You ready to give it a try?" he asked.

The girl took a deep breath and nodded.

Colt stood and led the way over to Destiny, keeping track of Margaret's hesitant steps behind him. When they reached the horse, he took the lead and rubbed the mare's muscular neck.

"Destiny's real friendly and loves attention." Colt swept his hand over the horse's back. "It always helps to introduce yourself before you ride. Wanna come over and let her get a good look at you?"

Margaret crept closer and Colt waited as her eyes roved over Destiny, starting with the horse's broad nose, then trailing down her thick midsection to her slowly flicking tail.

"She's big," she mumbled.

"Yeah. But she's safe." Colt nodded toward Destiny's muzzle. "Hold your hand up and let her get acquainted with your scent."

His sister raised her hand, stepping closer hesitantly. Destiny dipped her head and nudged Margaret's palm with her nose, nostrils working.

Margaret pulled back, cradled her hand to her chest and laughed. "That tickles."

Colt smiled. "Come closer and pet her."

She did, barely brushing her fingers against the horse's hide. After a few minutes, Margaret grew bolder, touching Destiny with her whole palm and applying long strokes along her shoulder. Destiny made a sound of pleasure and nuzzled her nose against Margaret's hair.

"She likes you, Margaret," Kayden said, walking his horse in a wide circle around them.

"Does she?" Margaret asked, looking up at Colt.

He nodded and gestured toward the saddle. "Ready to mount?"

Margaret glanced over her shoulder at Jen.

"Go ahead." Jen smiled and nodded. "We're right here with you, Margaret."

The girl inhaled and squared her shoulders. "Okay."

Colt helped hook her left foot in the stirrup, gripped her waist and boosted her up. He kept his hands at her sides as she straightened.

"All right?" he asked.

Margaret nodded jerkily, her small hands grappling for the saddle horn and holding it tightly.

"We'll just stand still a minute and let you get used to her," he added, slowly removing his hands and reaching for Destiny's lead.

His stomach churned as Margaret shifted slightly in the saddle. Her torso bent forward, her fingers scrambling for a death grip on the saddle horn. She looked so small up there on Destiny. So light and frail.

Colt shot a worried glance at Jen, his hands clenching on the reins. Dominic had assured him Destiny was the best choice for Margaret. But maybe he should've started with one of the small ponies no matter how big a blow to Margaret's newfound pride that might've been. Or maybe he should never have agreed to this at all.

"You look great up there," Jen said, issuing an encouraging smile. "Like a real cowgirl. Don't you think so, Colt?"

"Yeah." He cleared his throat. "You look great."

Colt licked his lips, his mouth suddenly dry. A familiar anxiety ran through him. The same one he experienced every time Jen positioned Diamond in the alley, preparing to tear around barrels at top speed. It was an irrational fear but he couldn't shake it.

"Wanna walk around with us, Margaret?" Kayden asked, continuing his slow circle around Destiny. "We'll go slow."

"Yeah," Jayden said, joining his brother. "There ain't nothing to it."

"Wait, boys—"

Before Colt could finish, Destiny took a few steps across the grass, following in line with the other horses as she did routinely during her daily trail rides with guests.

Margaret gasped, a panicked cry escaping her. "C-Colt?"

Heart lurching to his throat, he tugged on the reins and brought Destiny to a halt. He reached up and wrapped one hand around both of Margaret's on the saddle horn.

"Hey," he said gently. "You just say the word and I'll get you down. You've done a lot today already."

Margaret's wide, brown eyes moved over his face, then settled on his hand. Her breathing slowed and she tugged one hand free of the saddle horn to clutch his. Her small fingers twined with his larger ones and squeezed.

"Will you stay right here?" she asked.

"Of course."

She sat up straighter and nodded, the sunlight gleaming off her pink helmet and golden strands of hair rippling over her back. "Then I'm okay. We can keep going."

Colt's chest swelled, a surge of pride rising in him at the brave light in his sister's eyes. He nodded and tugged Destiny's reins, guiding her forward slowly. The first few steps were rocky, but after a few minutes, the anxious set of Margaret's mouth eased.

"Wonderful job, Margaret," Jen called out as they moved farther out across the field.

They continued in silence for a while, listening to the birds chirp overhead and the ranch guests laugh softly as they strolled the grounds nearby. Margaret sat taller in the saddle with each of Destiny's steps, causing Colt's smile to widen.

"See, it ain't so bad," Kayden said. "You like it?"

"Yeah." Margaret laughed. "We're doing good, aren't we, Colt?"

*We.* That word again. And just as sweet.

The rush of pleasure sweeping through Colt caught him by surprise. It bloomed in his chest and pooled in his eyes. He blinked rapidly, clearing his vision to absorb Margaret's bright, adoring smile.

"We sure are," he said.

Colt concentrated on the warm press of Margaret's palm, the strong surge of peace enveloping him suddenly giving the word new meaning. One he had let go of long ago. Something he'd finally stopped begging for from his father seven years ago, when he'd left home.

*Family.*

His hand tightened around his sister's, the rhythmic pulse in her wrist fluttering against his thumb.

Other than Tammy, Colt couldn't remember the last time he'd touched someone with his blood running through their veins. And it'd been years since he'd laid eyes on a face with as strong a resemblance to his own. He'd never experienced a moment of solidarity as powerful and unconditional as this before with anyone...

Except Jen. For a brief while last night in that guest room bed. When he'd joined his body to hers and settled into her comforting embrace, her tender touch dissolving his grief and infusing him with strength.

Margaret's head swiveled to the side, her shiny helmet flashing in the sunlight as she called out, "Colt and I are doing good, aren't we, Ms. Jen?"

"Fantastic," she shouted back, waving from the other side of the pasture.

Colt craned his neck, peering past Margaret. Jen had turned away to lean against the fence, her curvy profile highlighted by the low-hanging sun and her gaze focused on an adjacent field, where Diamond frolicked with the other horses.

Jen's name hovered on Colt's tongue, the need to bring her attention back to him strong. He wanted to call her over to share the moment. Ask her to join him. Take her hand in his and tug her close to his side.

But he couldn't. Both his hands were already full. One gripped Destiny's reins and the other still clasped Margaret's hand tightly, supporting and urging her on. And at the moment, his sister's needs were more important than his own.

## Chapter 8

Eight seconds of being thrown around by an angry bull had always taken a toll on Colt. But it was nothing compared to the four hours he'd spent waiting for Margaret to return safely from a neighbor's mid-morning pool party.

"They're late getting back," Colt said, hopping off the lowered tailgate of his truck.

He walked to the middle of Raintree's dirt driveway and peered down the winding lane, hoping to catch a glimpse of a truck emerging over the hill. A strong breeze swept across the grounds, spiraling up dust, then blowing through the long blades of grass in the fields.

"Kayden and Jayden have the ability to make anyone late," Dominic said, leaning against the side of the truck. "They've perfected it into an art form." He crunched into a large apple, chewed then swallowed before adding, "The Grangers may be our closest neighbors, but they're miles from here and they've got five kids of their own, plus however many children they invited to this party. That's enough to throw anyone's time off. Logan would've called if anything serious had happened. The kids are fine."

Colt nodded. Dominic's brother, Logan, was the most responsible man on the planet and he'd offered to pick the kids up on the way back from town. Logically, Colt should have nothing to worry about. Emotionally, however, well…that was a different story.

After a full afternoon of riding Destiny yesterday, Margaret had played cards with the boys, then stayed up late to watch a movie. She'd settled in between Colt and Jen on the couch and laughed often. But the long day had caught up with her, causing her blond head to tip onto Colt's chest and her snores to overpower the TV.

Colt rubbed a palm over the base of his throat, recalling the soft press of Margaret's hair as she'd slept. "Even if you know they're okay, don't you still worry about the boys when you're not with them?"

"Hell, yeah. Every day. Why else did you think Cissy and I took up residence out here a half hour ago?" Dominic asked, taking another bite of the apple. "Worrying is just part of being a parent. Part of wanting to keep your family safe. But wearing a hole in the driveway isn't gonna get 'em here any faster. Work's about the only thing that helps ease the stress while I'm waiting." His smile was only half-joking. "You given any more thought to my offer? 'Cause that'd keep your mind busy."

Colt ducked his head and looked away, focusing on the driveway again. It was nothing unusual for Dominic to reference his proposal that Colt partner up with him and Logan and invest in bulls. He'd mentioned it every time Colt visited over the past two years, and again when he'd arrived at Raintree with Margaret and Jen.

Dominic had given up bull riding years ago for Cissy and the boys, and had never looked back. But Colt knew Dominic still harbored a love for the sport. And Logan, shrewd businessman that he was, saw an investment in bulls and riding clinics as another opportunity for Raintree to grow.

"I've thought about it," Colt murmured.

He *had* thought about it. Much more often during this visit than he had before.

He'd thought about what it'd be like to slow down. Take more than one week off from touring the circuit. Give his body time to rest and heal from all the damage he'd done grappling with bulls over the years.

He'd also thought about Margaret. How staying longer would give him more time with her. Delay their separation and strengthen the new connection he'd begun to establish with her.

"It feels good walking across the dirt instead of slamming into it," Dominic said. "We'd be advising more than anything. Guiding newbies through the tricks of the trade. There's nothing wrong with slowing down. It's a hell of a lot more peaceful than dragging everything you own from one state to another every week."

The thundering of hooves erupted from an adjacent field. Diamond's white mane rippled along his back as Jen drove him around barrels.

Colt's mouth twisted. Jen hadn't slowed

down. Despite their long day yesterday, she had saddled Diamond up at dawn and spent the entire day conditioning and bonding. Every time Colt sought her out she'd been either in the fields or in the stable with Diamond. And the only time she'd offered more than a one-word response to him was when Margaret had come to hug her goodbye before leaving for the pool party.

Colt looked down and dragged his boot over the dirt. He'd hoped after Margaret left for the party that he'd have an opportunity to talk to Jen. To try to discuss the night they'd shared and explain that even though he knew he should focus on Margaret, he was finding it difficult to ignore how he felt about her. He needed to know if Jen felt as strongly for him.

But would he just be causing Jen more pain by restarting something he wasn't sure he could finish?

Delighted babbles rang out, interrupting Colt's thoughts. Dominic's twin girls stood outside the fence with Cissy, watching Jen and Diamond. Gwen's squeals of excitement cut across the peaceful spring air each time Diamond executed a turn, but Grace was oblivious to it. She was busy doing her best to climb the fence rails.

"No, Grace," Cissy said, catching the toddler as she lost her grip on the second rail and toppled toward the ground. "You'll fall and hurt yourself."

Grace let loose a plaintive shriek, threw her arms up and writhed in Cissy's hold, her ruffled shirt rising above her protruding belly as she slithered free to the ground.

Diamond balked at the piercing sound, jerking his head and skittering out of the barrel pattern to trot in the opposite direction.

"Whatcha giving your mama such a hard time for?" Dominic asked, tossing his apple core away and ambling over to scoop Grace up in his arms.

Cissy smiled, mouthing *thank you* as Dominic bent to kiss her cheek before returning to Colt's truck with Grace in tow.

"All that hollerin' isn't going to get you anywhere." Dominic gently tickled the tips of Grace's toes, peeking out of her sandals.

The little girl's screams ceased and a grin broke across her face. She kicked at Dominic's fingers and laughed.

"There's my good girl." Dominic kissed her forehead and hugged her to his chest.

Grace laid her cheek on his shoulder as he

rocked her from side to side, her blue eyes blinking up at Colt.

Colt shifted uncomfortably and looked away, but when he glanced back, the child's attention was still planted on him. She bounced in her dad's hold and yelped.

Dominic leaned back and smiled. "You want to visit with Colt a minute?"

Aw, hell. Colt didn't know the first thing about holding a baby. He froze as Grace's tiny hand stretched toward him, her fingers grasping for his arm.

"How 'bout it, Colt?" Dominic asked, leaning with Grace as she reached for him.

Colt held up a hand and shook his head. "Nah. I don't want—"

Grace cut him off, yelping in frustration and straining harder to grab his arm. Her face contorted.

Colt cringed. He knew that look. Temper tantrum time.

"Come on, man," Dominic said, laughing. "She just wants to get to know you, that's all."

Grace held her breath, her cheeks almost turning purple.

"All right," Colt grunted. "But just for a minute."

Dominic transferred Grace to Colt's arms,

the toddler's bottom settling in the crook of his elbow, her hands grabbing hunks of his shirt.

She stared at him again. Silently. Her rapid breaths puffing in and out of her rosebud mouth.

"Hey," Colt whispered.

Grace smiled, baby teeth on full display.

"Say hi to Mr. Colt," Dominic directed, grinning.

"Hi, Col'," Grace said.

Colt's mouth twitched as Grace released his shirt then patted his cheeks. She leaned in and hugged his neck, the light scent of baby shampoo releasing with her movements.

A wave of warmth flooded Colt's chest and he squeezed her gently in return.

Grace lifted her head and chortled up at him, her bright eyes shining.

"She's got a beautiful laugh," Colt said.

A hand clapped his back. "Just one of those makes all the struggles of being a parent worth it," Dominic said. "As soon as you hear it, you forget whatever frustrations came before. That's another benefit to hanging around here. You're able to spend quality time with people you care about. Time that's not squeezed in between eight-second intervals and weeks of driving."

Grace bounced and babbled, jostling Colt's arms and pointing.

Colt smiled as he wound a finger in one of her raven curls, the softness of it reminding him so much of Margaret's. "What is it?"

"I think she wants me," Jen said, her long legs carrying her gracefully to his side.

Colt swallowed hard. *I can understand that*. He tore his eyes from Jen's shapely figure and caught a glimpse of Diamond being led off by a stable hand. "You finished for the day?" he asked, his hopes resurfacing.

Maybe there'd still be a chance for him to coax her into a talk, after all.

She shrugged and drew closer, rubbing a hand over Grace's back. "I had a lot more planned, but *someone*," she teased, tapping the little girl's nose, "broke our concentration."

Grace babbled in a high-pitched voice and threw her arms out, grabbing for Jen.

Jen tugged her gently from Colt's arms, then settled the baby on her hip. "Just what are we gonna do with you, gorgeous?" She shook her head. "You're a handful and a half."

"Tell me about it," Dominic said, his voice tinged with amusement.

Jen lifted Grace in the air and blew raspberries against her belly, causing the baby's laughter to escalate into breathless squeals.

"Oh, I forgive you," Jen said, settling her back on her hip and kissing her rosy cheeks.

Colt's smile slipped. It was a breathtaking sight, Jen cradling Grace in her arms, pressing light kisses to her face, the spring breeze billowing her hair out in fiery waves around them.

A tingle started in Colt's middle and traveled upward, heating his chest and making his eyes heavy.

He'd never imagined it before. What a child would look like in Jen's arms.

Oh, he'd known it'd be a given one day. Jen was a keeper. The kind of woman you married and stayed committed to for a lifetime. And a man would be a fool if he didn't want her carrying his baby at some point along the way.

But the thought of Jen having another man's child hit Colt hard in the gut, causing him to suck in a breath between clenched teeth. For some reason, the possibility no longer sat right with him, and it sure as hell didn't fit the images he had in his mind. The ones that had formed the moment Jen bent to cuddle Grace.

The vision of a little boy with red hair just as bright and vibrant as Jen's, his personality as charming and feisty as hers, and blue eyes the same shade as—

Colt stilled, the realization fully forming. Blue eyes the same shade as his own. The child's entire makeup a perfect blend of his and Jen's best attributes, inside and out.

"Ah, here come the rest of the rascals now," Dominic said, tipping his chin toward the driveway. "Told you everything was fine."

Colt tore his eyes away from Jen, grateful for the distraction.

A large truck traveled slowly up the driveway, the rotating tires kicking up dust until it pulled to a stop in front of them. The passenger door opened and Kayden and Jayden sprang out of the backseat of the crew cab. Margaret exited next and her eyes were as bright as her smile.

"Guess what, Mr. Colt?" Kayden asked, bounding to his side. "The Grangers had a basketball hoop so it was a pool *and* basketball party." He paused, rubbing at his eyes as the dusty wind pushed him back on his heels for a moment. "We did one of those scrummage things."

"You mean *scrimmage*?" Colt asked, biting back a laugh.

"Yeah, that." Kayden waved away the correction, then punctuated the air with his hand. "But the thing is, it was mostly boys, right? 'Cause—"

"'Cause the girls didn't want to play," Jayden said, moving to his brother's side.

"Yeah, the girls didn't want to play," Kayden added. "None of 'em except—"

"Margaret," Jayden said. "Margaret was the only girl at the pool party that played—"

"Oh, hush up, Jayden." Kayden stamped his foot. "I'm telling it, okay?"

"All right, all right." His twin made a face, then bounded off toward the front of the truck.

Kayden smirked, shaking his head. "Anyways, Margaret was the only girl that played. And guess what?" He paused for emphasis, brows raising and mouth widening. "She made every shot she took and whopped every one of the boys." He hesitated, frowning, then straightened. "'Cept for me and Jayden. She didn't beat us."

"Yes, I did," Margaret said, her smile stretching from ear to ear. "I scored seventeen more points than both of you."

Kayden rolled his eyes and shrugged. "All right. She made more baskets than us. But she wasn't as fast as we were. *And* she didn't steal the ball as much as we did."

Margaret cocked her head to the side. "That's true."

Colt laughed and squeezed his sister's shoulder. "That's fantastic, Margaret. I'm proud of you."

"Thanks." She blushed, then skipped past him to greet Jen and coo up at Grace.

A door slammed on the truck and Logan ambled around to the other side, Jayden following close at his heels.

"So can we, Uncle Logan?" the boy pleaded. "It's windy enough today."

"Well, I suppose one early birthday gift wouldn't hurt," Logan said, grinning.

A tall, raven-haired woman slid out from the front passenger seat and ruffled Jayden's blond hair. "The kites were supposed to be a surprise. I bought them in town for the boys' birthday before we went to pick them up, and thought I'd hidden them pretty well." She laughed, glancing at Colt. "But I guess I didn't do as good a job as I thought."

"We'll pretend we didn't see 'em if you want us to, Aunt Amy," Jayden said, his expression dimming. "But it sure is a perfect day to fly a kite."

"Their birthday's tomorrow, babe," Logan said, kissing his wife's neck as he eased around her to reach into the cab. "And today's as good a day as any."

"Oh, all right." Amy's expression warmed as Logan emerged from the cab with a dark-haired baby in his arms.

Colt smiled. Dominic had told him that Logan and Amy had reconciled some time ago after a prolonged separation, and had had a child. Judging from the warm glances they exchanged over the smiling boy in Logan's arms, and the closeness they'd displayed since Colt's arrival, he could tell they were happy and very much in love.

They'd created the same kind of strong family Dominic and Cissy had made. The kind Colt found himself admiring more with each passing day at Raintree.

"Well," Logan said, cupping a broad palm against the baby's cheek to block the wind. "If we're gonna do this, we better get this show on the road while the breeze is still blowing."

Margaret, Kayden and Jayden squealed.

They huddled together and pointed to various areas of a nearby field, each laying claim to a corner. Colt lowered the tailgate of the truck and he and Dominic unpacked the kites.

The women chatted and laughed, Cissy and Gwen having joined the group, and it wasn't long before Jen held baby Ethan on her hip with one arm and wrapped the other one around Grace, who clung to her leg. The babies giggled and bounced in Jen's embrace, basking in her attention.

Colt's eyes hovered on Jen, that warm buzz returning to his middle and heating his face. The feeling, though pleasant, unsettled him. He'd never imagined being this at ease surrounded by babies and kids. But the comforting family atmosphere made him long for children of his own and led him to imagine new possibilities. Ones that would allow him to provide the support Margaret needed but also enable him to build a real relationship with Jen.

The notion made him reconsider Dominic's offer. And it also spurred thoughts of a different kind of partnership.

One that had nothing to do with Dominic's business venture but everything to do with Jen.

* * *

"Don't let it get away!"

A laugh burst from Jen's chest, her lungs aching as she gasped for air and kept her eyes glued to the white string flicking through the lush blades of grass. She pumped her legs harder, running faster across the field and casting occasional looks at the colorful parafoil kite whisking higher into the blue sky. Colt's and Margaret's boots made swishing sounds through the grass behind her as they struggled to catch the runaway toy.

"We can't let it get away," Margaret squealed again.

Her voice faded more with each of Jen's sprinting steps. Jen pried her attention away from the string long enough to glance back at Colt. He nipped at her heels, but his breath wasn't coming half as fast as hers. And his grin had a smug tilt to it.

She faced forward again and sped up, ignoring the desire pooling in her belly, and focusing on the burning sensation in her thighs instead.

"Watch out, Jen!"

Colt's concerned tone swept across her neck, raising goose bumps that chased each other down her spine. She swung her arms faster, quickened her pace and kept tabs on the escaping kite.

"Jen."

"Wha—"

Her heel hit a gopher hole, twisting her ankle and stealing her balance.

Colt's caught her upper arm and pulled her, keeping her from slamming to the ground. But his feet tangled with hers and they fell, anyway, Colt landing on his back with her clutched to his side.

Jen lay winded for a moment, gasping for breath. The thin string snaked away with a whisper and the kite soared above the tree line. Each flap of its tie-dyed wings beat in time with the pounding of Colt's heart beneath her palm, and the hard length of his thigh against hers sent a wave of heat through her.

A round of cheers echoed across the field and Jen shifted her head to the side, her cheek pressing against the grass. The Slade family waved from their position on the far side, where the boys were trying to outrun each other, their kites flapping behind them, and the adults were helping the younger ones hold on to their strings. They were all smiles and good-natured teasing.

Laughter escaped Jen. She looked back at Colt, his sexy smile shooting a delicious thrill through her. "Seems we're the entertainment for the afternoon. And all because you were too slow."

Colt's broad chest shook with deep chuckles. "Now, don't blame it on me. You're the one that caused the wreck." His laughter dissolved and his blue eyes darkened as they dropped to her mouth. "Jen. I wanted to—"

A strong *oof* erupted from Colt's lips as a small body landed on his middle.

Margaret giggled breathlessly as she lay on him, blinking up at both of them with laughing eyes before she stated the obvious. "It got away."

Jen's breath stuck in her lungs at the surprised happiness on Colt's face.

He lifted his big hands and swept his sister's hair away from her fluttering lashes and laughing mouth. "It sure did."

Margaret propped her chin on Colt's chest and smiled. "Guess what? Mrs. Cissy said I can help cook supper tonight if I want to. They're making biscuits from scratch and she said they put honey butter on them after they come out of the oven." She glanced at Jen excitedly. "You'd like those, wouldn't you, Ms. Jen?"

Jen nodded and avoided Colt's eyes, the diversion coming at just the right time. "They sound delicious."

"Will you come help make them, too?"

"Sure." Jen held up a hand and wiggled it. "But you're gonna have to help me up first."

Margaret sprang to her feet and tugged at Jen until she stood. "Will you come, too, Colt?"

He sat up and brushed at the grass on his jeans. "Yep. Just as soon as I help pack up the kites."

Margaret hesitated. "Want us to wait for you?"

"Nah." Colt waved a hand. "Go ahead, Margaret. I'll catch up."

"Meg's okay," Margaret said.

Colt's hand stilled over his pant leg as he glanced up. "What?"

"You know." His sister bit her lip, her cheeks flushing. The breeze shifted a wispy curl across her face and she pushed it back. "If you still want to call me Meg, that'd be okay."

The warmth in Colt's blue eyes and Margaret's shy grin caused Jen's heart to turn over in her chest. And for a moment, she didn't want to go inside. Or anywhere else.

She had a strong desire to remain standing

in the green field between Colt and Margaret, skin heating beneath the glow of the sun and chest humming with the sweetness of the moment they shared.

Colt's chest rose on a deep breath. "I'd like that very much, Meg," he murmured.

Margaret's smile returned full blast and she grabbed Jen's hand and pulled. "Come on, Ms. Jen. Let's go make some biscuits."

It took about twenty minutes to gather the ingredients and mix the dough, and an additional half hour to cook them. But the frequent laughter and comforting warmth of the kitchen had Jen and Margaret staying for a lot longer. They dived into the preparations for the other dinner dishes, following the head chef's directions to the letter. Betty, Amy's mother, was the best cook in a ten-state radius and ran an organized kitchen. She was also a jubilant lady who gave snug hugs and kind praise for all their efforts.

It wasn't long before Cissy, Amy and Amy's younger sister, Traci, joined them. In two hours, they'd whipped up a spread worthy of a banquet. And by the time everyone was seated, the dining room was packed. The clink of ice in glasses and silverware against plates was steady. And so were the smiles.

The kids chatted nonstop about the boys' birthday and Logan told them he'd planned an outdoor movie night to celebrate the occasion. The kids approved, releasing delighted cheers and immediately talking about preparations.

The moment was welcoming and warm, but the family atmosphere settling over the table stirred an ache in Jen's chest. An ache that throbbed long after dinner was over and must've shown on her face, causing Colt's eyes to find her several times.

After helping Betty clear the table, Jen excused herself and headed for the door. The warm night air cradled her bare arms as she made her way down the steps, the crickets' and cicadas' rhythmic chirps pulsing around her. She hesitated, slipping her hand in her pocket and running her thumb over the edge of her cell phone.

"Taking a walk?"

Jen glanced over her shoulder. Colt stood on the front porch, brow creasing with concern.

"Yeah," she said, rubbing her palms over her jeans. "Thought I'd check out the old barn on the back lot. Cissy said there's a good view from the hayloft."

His features relaxed and he rocked back on

his heels. "That sounds like a plan. Mind if I join you?" He nodded toward the house. "I'm gonna check on Meg and make sure she's settled. Then I could grab us a beer on the way out."

Jen smiled slightly at the way his voice lingered over Margaret's nickname. He'd repeated it all night when he'd spoken to her, as though holding the syllable on his tongue to savor it.

"It'd give us a chance to talk." He hesitated, voice lowering. "I was wrong about the way I left things between us and I want to hear what you think. See if we can work out a way to move forward together. I'd really like to talk, Jen."

Jen bit her lip hard, but nodded. "Okay." Her voice caught and she cleared her throat. "I'm gonna go ahead."

The worried glint returned to his blue eyes, but he turned, heading back into the house and saying over his shoulder, "I'll be right behind you."

Jen took her time navigating the winding trail to the old barn. The moon was full and its white glow lit up the wide fields and spilled over the dirt path.

She spotted the large barn at the end of the

trail, its angular shape outlined against the backdrop of stars. The spring sun had set, but the bright night sky highlighted the building and surrounding grounds with soft light.

Weathered wood squeaked on its hinges as she pushed the barn door open. Jen inhaled the sweet scent of hay and musty aroma of age hanging in the air. She climbed the rickety ladder, hitching her legs carefully over gaps left by missing rungs, then settled onto a pile of loose hay at the edge of the loft.

She tugged her cell phone from her pocket and dialed, holding her breath until the long succession of rings stopped.

"Hello?"

The voice droning over the line was hoarse with sleep and tinged with irritation.

Jen sat up straighter. "Hi, Mom."

A beat of silence was followed by a rustling sound. "Jen? What's happened? Are you all right?"

"I'm fine, Mom. Nothing's happened."

Jen swung her legs nervously, bumping the back of her calves against the loft's ledge. A fresh wave of shame swept through her. She couldn't blame her mom for the anxious reaction. It'd been over three years since she'd last called her. And calling, then almost immediately saying goodbye each time, had eventually become too painful to continue. So she'd stopped phoning altogether.

"I just..." Jen pulled in a shaky breath. "I just wanted to hear your voice."

Nora's sigh drifted over the phone. "I'm glad to hear your voice, too. But you scare me to death calling this time of night, Jen."

Jen clutched the phone tighter, her stomach churning. It'd been late the night the call had come years ago, notifying Jen's mother that her husband had been in a car accident. Jen couldn't remember much from that night, she'd been so young. But she did recall how hard her mother's fingers had trembled when she'd buttoned Jen's coat and hustled her outside to make the trip to the hospital.

"I know," Jen said, guilt gnawing at her insides. "I'm sorry. I just thought I'd check in. See how you're doing."

"I'm fine," Nora said, her tone hard and heavy with the grit of tough living. "Always am. Where are you?"

"Back in Georgia." Jen hesitated. "I'm taking a break from the circuit."

"A permanent break?" Her mom's tone lifted. "Are you coming home?"

"No." Jen forced out the words. "I'm just

helping out a—" she swallowed hard "—a friend for a few days. Then I'm going back. So I won't have time to visit, but I promise I will once this tour is over."

Nora was silent for a moment before saying, "You've been roaming the road for a long time now, Jen. Whatever it is you're looking for, you're not going to find it out there. Thought you'd have learned that by now."

Jen stilled, reminding herself of the rewards all the hard work would eventually bring.

"I'm an athlete, Mom. If I want to be successful, I have to make sacrifices. Traveling is just part of the life."

"I suppose. But I still think you do too much of it," Nora said softly. "The girls asked about you the other day. They look for you on the box from time to time."

The girls. Jen smiled. The women that bused tables with her mother had always gotten a kick out of her rodeo tales during her rare visits home. And "the box" was an old, beat-up TV barely clinging to the wall above the bar at The Greasy Spoon.

"Tell them to keep watching," Jen said. "Because they're going to see me win a title soon."

"Jen, how long are you going to do this?" Her mom's voice gentled. "I know I'm hard on you, but I keep at you because I love you. You've wasted years already, and if you're not careful you're going to use up the best ones you've got left chasing something that will never happen—"

"It *will* happen," Jen said. "I'm good at what I do and I'm going to win big soon."

"There's an opening at the diner. I could put in a good word for you."

"I'm not coming back to Hollow Rock to break my back wiping scraps off dirty tables and trying to live off crumpled dollar bills like—"

Jen clamped her mouth shut and closed her eyes, dismay heating her face.

"Like me, you mean?"

Her shoulders slumped. "I'm so sorry, Mom. I didn't mean it that way," she whispered. "But please try to understand. It's just...you know nothing's ever come easy for me. Except racing. It's the only thing I've ever been any good at." Her throat tightened. "I'm a joke in Hollow Rock. But on the circuit, Diamond and I shine, Mom. We stand out. I'm someone important that people notice and remember. Someone you can be proud of. And when I win, I'll be able to take care of both of us. I'll be able to get you out of Hollow Rock."

"I've been proud of you every day of your life, Jen. And I'm doing fine here. I've never needed anything more than what I got right now. Except for maybe seeing my daughter more often." Her voice turned brusque. "I gotta go. I'm working the graveyard shift tonight and a double tomorrow. I need to snag sleep when I can. Be careful out there."

"Mom?" Jen clutched the phone harder, straining to hear something other than silence, her vision blurring. "You and the girls keep watching the box, okay? You're going to see me soon."

Nora's voice broke on her next words. "I'd rather see you in person, Jen."

The phone clicked and the line went dead.

Jen looked up at the sparkling sky, the stars winking and the moon bigger than she'd ever seen it. Transfixed, she reminded herself how much more there was outside Hollow Rock and Raintree Ranch. How much more to experience and how much easier she'd be able to make her mother's life after earning a good reputation and enough money to support them both. And how hard she'd worked to become someone that mattered.

"You okay?"

Jen jumped and glanced over her shoulder, blinking rapidly to clear the tears from her eyes and shoving the phone back in her pocket.

Colt stood a few feet away.

"Yeah." Jen faced forward, swallowing the lump in her throat. "Just touching base with home."

"Everything all right there?" Colt asked, sitting beside her.

"Same as always," she said drily.

"I can be a good listener." He nudged her with his shoulder. "Want to talk about it?" He pressed something cold into her hand.

"Not particularly." Jen narrowed her eyes. "What's this?"

"A juice box."

She glanced at him and raised a brow.

He shrugged, mouth twitching. "They were out of beer and it was the easiest thing to grab. It's grape."

They unwrapped their straws and drank their juice in silence. "Not as refreshing as a beer, but pretty good, huh?" He laughed at her nod and shook his head slowly, saying, "How things have changed."

Jen stilled, a trickle of dread creeping

through her at his thoughtful expression. Things *had* begun to change. No matter how much she tried to forget.

Jen longed to lay her head on his chest again. To feel the warm swell of emotion when he touched her. And she longed for the feeling of family she'd experienced this afternoon. The carefree sound of Margaret's laughter earlier had her palms itching to grab another kite and chase it across the field again. To feel that surge of affection when Margaret smiled, and savor the comforting squeeze of her small hand inside Jen's own.

Jen frowned. It was Raintree's doing. The family atmosphere had stirred an ache of homesickness through her blood, prompting her to call home for the first time in ages. And the strengthening attraction she shared with Colt, plus the new connection she'd formed with Margaret, threatened to steal her focus from racing and make her forget...

*Vegas.* Tammy. All the years Jen had spent apart from her mother. Everything she'd sacrificed so far. How ridiculous she'd look if she failed now, all the hard work in vain if she quit.

She froze, realizing that Colt and Margaret had become more important than checking stats and training. More important than winning and earning a name for herself. And every day she spent at Raintree threatened to derail her resolve to return to the circuit.

"I need to compete," Jen said, dropping the juice box. "I checked the stats last night and I'm twelfth now."

Colt's smile melted away. "Twelfth's not bad, Jen."

"It's only four ranks away from not making the cut for Vegas and it'll keep dropping the longer I sit out." She straightened. "There's a competition in Springfield Saturday. There's a big pot and winning would really help me climb again."

Colt frowned and propped his elbows on his knees. "The boys' birthday is tomorrow." He rotated the juice box slowly between his strong hands, watching it turn. "Meg's looking forward to the party and we'd planned to stay until at least noon on Sunday."

"She won't miss the party. Springfield is only a three-hour drive from here, so I can wait until Saturday morning to leave." Jen hesitated, dragging her teeth over her bottom lip and wincing at the guilt rising within her. "I'll come back to Raintree Saturday night and stay Sunday if you want. But after that,

I've got to get back on the road. I'm losing my position and I need the wins." She touched his forearm, resisting the urge to wrap her fingers around it, and whispered, "You promised, Colt."

He glanced up, his troubled eyes roving slowly over her face. "I did promise, didn't I?" A tight smile appeared and he reached out, tucking a strand of hair behind her ear and brushing his knuckles gently over her cheek. "Okay, Red. We'll go to Springfield Saturday."

Jen pulled away and looked at the sky, trying to ignore the warm press of Colt's arm against her own and the pleasant sensations fluttering in her chest. She avoided any further conversation, concentrating on the race and the fact that Colt had agreed to make the trip with her. And tried not to linger over the painful thought of leaving Margaret the day after.

# Chapter 9

*Flirty Fuchsia or Romantic Rose?*

Jen stood in the middle of the bedroom, reading the label on a tube of lipstick in each hand. Flirty Fuchsia was more a light shade of pink than purple, so it was always a good fit with her warm skin tone. But the red in Romantic Rose matched her hair exactly and really made her lips pop—

*Wait.* Jen clenched her fists around the lipstick tubes. *This is a children's birthday party.* An outdoor movie night with mosquitoes, gnats and squealing toddlers running all over the place. It was *not* a flirty or romantic occasion. And it certainly wasn't an opportunity to tempt Colt into touching her again…

*I was wrong about the way I left things between us and I want to hear what you think. See if we can work out a way to move forward together.*

She sighed as she recalled Colt's words, her cheek tingling from the remembered feel of his fingers brushing against her skin. It'd been almost a day since they'd sat in the hayloft, sipping from juice boxes and watching the stars, but she still couldn't shake the effect he had on her. Which made it harder than ever to forget the night they'd spent together, and even more difficult to keep her distance from him.

On more than one occasion this morning, she'd found herself inching closer to Colt's side as they'd watched Margaret ride Destiny across the field, his sister's trust in the horse having increased tremendously.

And Jen's pulse had tripped every time she'd caught Colt's eyes lingering on her mouth as they'd blown up balloons for the boys' birthday party.

Which, she reluctantly acknowledged, might account for why she was so dang fixated on which shade of color would dress up her lips more, when she should be focused on prepping for the race in Springfield tomorrow night. The one that could make or break her ability to hold on to her spot in the top fifteen.

"Vegas," she whispered, shaking her head.

That was where her attention needed to be. Not on Colt. No matter how tempted she was to give in to his suggestion to reconsider their relationship.

"Wow! You look really pretty, Ms. Jen."

Margaret flicked the light off in the en suite bathroom and walked over, her eyes widening as they drifted over Jen.

A familiar affection stirred within Jen. She and Margaret had had a rough start sharing the guest room. The girl's snores and Jen's fondness for long soaks in the tub had caused irritation for both of them. But a pair of earplugs and a daily bathroom schedule had solved those problems the second day, and Jen had enjoyed Margaret's company the rest of the week.

No. More than that. Whispers and giggles with Margaret each evening had become endearing, and sneaking a glimpse of Margaret peacefully sleeping first thing in the morning had become a pleasant start to each day.

Margaret reached out, touching Jen's

sleeveless turquoise blouse, then rubbed the silky material between her thumb and forefinger. "I like this," she said.

"Thank you." Jen smiled, admiring Margaret's ruffled tank top and dressy jeans. The pink butterflies sewn below the pockets matched her designer boots. "You look nice, too. I like what you've put together."

Margaret grinned, stuck her arms out and spun in a circle, her long hair swinging in a wide arc. "Ms. Trudy said it's authentic—"

"Western wear," Jen finished for her, laughing. "Indeed, it is."

Margaret stopped spinning and eyed Jen's hands. "What's that?"

Jen showed her. "Lipstick." She shook her head. "Not that there's any real need for it."

Margaret sprang forward and plucked the tubes from her hands, then uncapped each one. "Oh, I like this one better," she gushed, thrusting out the Romantic Rose and eyeing Jen's mouth.

Jen hesitated. Romance should not be on the agenda tonight. But the thought of sharing a few more precious moments with Colt was tempting. And the excited gleam in Margaret's eyes won out.

Jen faced the dresser mirror and swept the

color over her lips, trying not to smile as the little girl poked her head in close, her face appearing in the reflection.

Margaret's brown eyes tilted upward, clinging to the movements of Jen's hand.

Jen finished applying the lipstick, rubbed her lips together a few times, then glanced at Margaret. "There. How does it look? Is it even?"

She nodded, smiling. "Can I wear some?"

Jen shook her head. "I think this color is a bit too dark for you."

Margaret's features fell. "Okay," she whispered.

"But," Jen said, digging out a slim tube from her makeup bag on the dresser, "I have a lip gloss that I think would suit you perfectly."

Margaret's face brightened and she took it eagerly, taking off the cap and smiling at the tinted stick. "It's pink."

"Yep. Give it a try."

Margaret stepped close to the mirror, parted her mouth and made careful sweeps across her lips, mimicking Jen's movements exactly.

When finished, she put the top back on and looked up at Jen. "How's that?"

Jen smiled. "Perfect."

"Can I have some blush, too?" Margaret's hands shot out for the makeup bag. "And eye shadow and mascara?"

"Oh, no." Jen laughed, squatting in front of her and stilling her hands. "Let's not get carried away." She squeezed the girl's fingers. "You're naturally beautiful. Besides, you've got a lot of years to wear all that stuff and it can become a real aggravation after a while. So let's not rush it, okay?"

"Does it aggravate you? Putting on makeup?"

"Yep," Jen said. "So does tweezing and waxing and conditioning…" She shrugged. "And all the other ten thousand things a woman does to look nice. Men have it easy and most of them don't even appreciate it." She wrinkled her nose. "The stinkers."

Margaret giggled and fiddled with a ruffle on her shirt. "Do boys like makeup on a girl?"

Jen smothered a grin at the pink flush blooming on Margaret's cheeks. Though she and the boys had played together as a trio over the past week, Margaret had begun to stick slightly closer to Kayden's side than Jayden's.

"Are you asking about a certain boy in particular?"

She shook her head rapidly, her hair spilling over her shoulders. "N-no. I was just wondering, you know?"

"I see." Jen tapped a finger under Margaret's chin and met her eyes. "A girl shouldn't make decisions based on what a boy wants. It's not important whether a boy likes a girl wearing makeup or not. What's important is whether or not *she* likes to wear it. Sometimes I like to put it on and sometimes I don't."

Margaret's eyebrows rose. "But you wanted to wear it tonight, right?"

Jen's face heated, her belly flipping at the thought of Colt's gaze lingering on her lips. She was suddenly overwhelmed with the desire to feel his mouth touching hers again, regardless of what regrets tomorrow might hold. "Yeah," she whispered. "I guess I did."

Margaret's smile returned. "I did, too."

"Well, that's all that matters then." Jen stood, ducked her head to hide her burning cheeks and zipped the makeup bag.

"Colt said he's taking you to a race tomorrow," Margaret said, leaning against the dresser and examining her boots.

"Yep." Jen put on a pair of stud earrings, then grabbed a comb and made adjustments to a few wayward strands of Margaret's hair. "In Springfield."

"Is that far away?"

Jen's hand paused over a blond curl. Margaret's question was so faint she barely caught it.

"Not too far," she said, putting the comb down and ignoring the uneasiness in her middle. "Colt has already talked to Mrs. Cissy about taking care of you while we're gone tomorrow afternoon, and we'll be back after you go to bed."

"Can I go, too?" Margaret pushed off the dresser and straightened. "I won't get in the way, I promise. And I don't get tired very easily, so you don't have to worry about getting me back in time for bed."

Jen hesitated. "Well, that's really up to Colt. He'll know what's best."

"But if it were up to you, would you let me go?"

Pleasure swept through Jen at the thought of seeking out Margaret's affectionate smile—so similar to Colt's—at the start of the race. And the thought of disappointing Margaret made it impossible for Jen to refuse.

"If it were up to me, I think I would." She held out a hand, avoiding Margaret's eyes and flinching at how much pain she'd cause the little girl when she had to leave for good. "Now, are you ready to head to the party?"

Margaret took her hand and hopped to her side. "Yep."

They each grabbed a brightly wrapped present from the bed and made their way outside, following the luminarias lining the winding path to the old barn. It was an ideal evening for an outdoor movie. A warm breeze whispered across Raintree's grounds, carrying the cheerful songs of frogs and crickets. The moon and stars were out in full force and even if the luminarias hadn't been in place, the two of them could've easily found their way by following the laughter hanging in the air.

"Wow."

Jen's heart tripped in her chest at the low comment, and she glanced up to find Colt standing at the end of the path, his eyes traveling slowly over her, his expression lifting with masculine approval.

*Vegas. Remember Vegas.* Jen held her breath and mentally ran through the barrel pattern.

"Doesn't she look great?" Margaret asked,

skipping up to his side. "I picked out the lipstick."

Colt blinked, glanced down at his sister, then cupped his palm to her cheek. "You did a good job. You both look beautiful."

"You clean up pretty well yourself," Jen said then cringed at the flirtatious, almost seductive note in her voice. She'd strived for flippancy but had failed miserably.

"Clean up" was an extreme understatement. She couldn't tear her eyes away from Colt. They clung to his broad shoulders and chest stretching a blue button-down shirt. They traveled over his slim-fitting jeans, the faded material hugging his hips and muscled thighs and creasing in the most enticing places.

"Thanks."

Her eyes shot back up to his face, and his sexy, lopsided grin made her cheeks heat right along with her blood.

His grin widened.

"Ms. Jen said I could go with y'all tomorrow if it's okay with you," Margaret said, tugging at her brother's arm.

"Oh, she did, did she?" Colt asked, surprised eyes darting back to Jen.

"Yep." His sister pulled at him harder. "So

can I go, Colt? I've never been to a race before."

He nodded, a pleased smile appearing as he examined Jen's face. "Yeah. It'd be nice to have you with us." He took Margaret's free hand, then turned to the side, bending his arm and gesturing with his elbow to Jen. "May I?"

Jen hesitated, the gentlemanly move one she'd never seen Colt make. One that matched his clean-shaven look and suited him far more than it should. She tried her best to refuse, but the tingling in her blood made her limbs move forward, anyway.

"You may," she whispered, shifting the birthday present to her other hand and slipping her arm through his.

His spicy male scent enveloped her and she pressed closer to his side as he escorted them across the open field toward the old barn. With each step, his strong leg brushed against her and his biceps flexed beneath her palm.

That tingling in her blood morphed into searing heat. It rushed through her veins and danced beneath her skin, making her long to slide her arms around him and press as close as possible. It tempted her to forget the race, stay at Raintree tomorrow and take him up on his offer to talk.

Jen pried her attention away from Colt and focused on the field ahead, admiring the setup. The doors of the old barn were shut and a large white sheet was tacked to it. A popular kids' cartoon projected onto the sheet from a machine propped on the lowered tailgate of a truck, and large speakers amplified the sound. Several hay bales were stacked into makeshift seating, draped with plaid blankets and arranged in a big semicircle in front of the barn. The balloons she and Colt had blown up were tied to each one and danced in the night breeze.

Guests had spread out blankets several feet in front of the hay bales and were propped up on pillows or seated on lawn chairs. A row of pickup trucks were parked at the back, tailgates down and pointed at the screen. Blankets and pillows were stacked in each and a red-and-white popcorn machine stood nearby, a steady stream of puffed kernels bouncing out of the silver cooking pot and piling high.

"Hey, Margaret."

Jen smiled as Kayden and Jayden bounded over, their blond hair tousled and lips stained punch red. They skipped to a breathless stop and gestured over their shoulders.

"Ain't it cool?" Kayden asked. "Uncle

Logan set up the movie and Uncle Dominic fixed all the hay bales and—"

"Aunt Amy did the popcorn," Jayden added.

"And there's punch and cake and—"

"All right, boys." Colt laughed. "Slow down or your motor is gonna run down halfway through the movie."

"Thanks for fixing up the trucks with the pillows, Mr. Colt," Jayden said.

"Yeah, thanks," Kayden added. "Can we sit in your truck, Mr. Colt? Aunt Cissy said we could as long as it was all right with you."

Colt smiled and nodded. "Sure. There should be enough room."

"Oh, we'll fit," Jayden said. "Hey…" His blue eyes drifted over the gifts in Jen's and Margaret's hands. "Are those for us, Ms. Jen?"

She laughed and nodded. "Sure are," she said, handing hers over. "Happy birthday, boys."

Margaret smiled, blushing as she placed her gift in Kayden's hands. "Happy birthday."

The boys said thanks and shook the boxes before putting them on a nearby table stacked high with presents.

"So, how old are you two now?" Colt asked

when they returned, squinting and tilting his head. "About six or seven?"

Kayden pursed his lips, amusement lighting his eyes as he clucked his tongue. "We ain't been six or seven for years, Mr. Colt."

Jayden shared a glance with his brother. They stuck out their chests, adopted deep voices and stated in unison, "We're nine."

They all laughed, then weaved their way through the scattered guests to Colt's truck, stopping along the way for popcorn and punch.

"All right," Colt said, setting all the snacks safely in the truck bed. "Ms. Jen and I'll hop up first and y'all can have the tailgate."

Colt climbed into the truck bed then leaned over, extending a strong hand. She slipped her hand in his, her palm tingling in his warm hold, and stepped up. She bit her lip as he grabbed her waist to steady her, his fingers tightening around her for a moment.

"You good?" he asked, trailing his hands away slowly.

"Yeah," she said, trying to ignore the flutters in her belly and taking a seat against the pillows at the back.

He nodded, then reached down and assisted Margaret up. The boys clambered onto the tailgate beside her. Once they were settled, Colt made sure the kids had their snacks before easing down beside Jen with a grunt.

"It's a chore keeping up with them, isn't it?" Jen teased, studying the three children's backs, their blond hair ruffling in the breeze.

Colt laughed. "I guess, but—"

Kids groaned and booed all over the field, drowning out the cheerful chatter of the adults, as the cartoon was cut off and the feature film was loaded. Children on the hay bales threw popcorn at the sheet until a new image flashed and the movie started, the booing quickly transforming into excited cheers as the opening music swelled.

Margaret and the boys joined in, whooping with the others. Kayden and Jayden tucked their popcorn bags at their sides and pumped the air with a fist. They whistled around their fingers, attention fixed on the movie and backs jerking with each of their movements.

"It might be a chore," Colt answered, raising his voice above the happy cries of the children and easing closer, "but it sure is a fun one."

A delicious shiver swept through Jen at the boyish tilt of his smile. No matter how much she tried to fight it, the magic of the moment slipped beneath her skin and lit her up inside. She closed her eyes, listening to the happy sounds of the children, and inhaled the rich scent of popcorn and butter lingering in the spring air.

"It is fun," she agreed, hugging her knees to her chest. "Kind of makes you feel like a kid again." She smiled and glanced at Colt, stilling as his blue eyes darkened.

"I wish I'd known you back then," he whispered.

Her breath caught and she cleared her throat before asking, "Why? So we could've raced our bikes? Or so you could've seen my skinned knees and buckteeth?"

Colt smiled. His hand lifted, halted in the air briefly, then drifted through her hair. "So I could've been the first boy to kiss you."

Something shifted in Jen's chest and settled firmly inside her heart. The phrase was softer and sweeter than any she'd ever imagined Colt would say to her. And she realized she finally knew the real Colt. An honest, honorable man she understood, had forgiven and trusted more than ever.

She melted beneath his touch, closing her eyes again and savoring the intoxicating feel of his presence surrounding her.

His lips brushed her ear and his gentle breaths tickled her skin. "May I?"

She tilted up her face and whispered back, "You may."

Her lips trembled, anticipating his kiss, but the soft heat of his mouth touched her neck instead, drifting slowly upward and brushing gently over her chin and the curves of each cheek.

His palms cradled her face, his thumbs gliding over her temples. "Jen."

The low syllable was coaxing and tinged with wonder. She opened her eyes to find him looking down at her, something new and different moving through his expression.

His mouth parted on a swift breath and he lowered his forehead to hers, eyes clinging to hers, his broad chest pressing warmly against her. "I—"

"Mr. Colt and Ms. Jen sitting in a tree..." Kayden's singsong voice faltered. "No, not a tree..."

Jen glanced to the side to find Margaret and the boys watching them. The twins sported goofy expressions and Margaret's smile was dreamy.

Kayden tried again, keeping time with his fist on the tailgate. "Sitting in a..."

Jen faced Colt again, her cheeks heating as she watched his eyes slide shut in dismay.

"Truck," Jayden hollered.

A smack sounded. "No, Jayden. That don't rhyme with *g*."

"Well, you can't say *tree* because they're not in one," Margaret said, giggling.

Colt shook his head and groaned, his chest vibrating against Jen's.

"I got it," Kayden declared, scrambling to his feet. He propped his hands on his hips and shouted, "Mr. Colt and Ms. Jen sitting at a moo-*vee*. *K-i-s-s-i-n-g!*"

Margaret and Jayden cackled and applauded. Kayden took a bow, then doubled over with laughter, attracting amused looks from the adults nearby.

"Oh, Lord," Jen murmured, covering her face.

Colt chuckled and tugged gently at her hands, removing them from her face and threading his fingers through hers. "Well," he said, "that certainly ruined the mood."

*Thank goodness.* One more moment and she would no longer have cared if she returned to the circuit. Her palms grew clammy, her fingers shaking between his. She tugged them free and shifted away, staring at the movie and avoiding Colt's eyes.

It wouldn't do to linger over the way he'd slipped into her blood, his gentle words and warm touch streaming through her veins and nourishing new feelings within her. Feelings that fought to dive deep inside her heart and take root, planting her feet and slowing her down. She needed every bit of speed she had to make her way to Vegas, and she'd worked too hard to throw it all away. But just for tonight, maybe she could enjoy these moments with Margaret and Colt.

Colt couldn't find the words for it. There was no phrase that fit the way Jen's arm had nestled so perfectly in the crook of his elbow or the way Margaret's hand settled so sweetly inside his own. But he felt it. It'd hummed within him the entire time they'd sat in the back of his truck, Meg giggling at the movie and Jen pretending to watch it. And that feeling stayed with him now as he escorted them back to the main house for the night.

Colt maneuvered them around a deep dip in the path, adjusting his grip around Margaret's hand and tugging Jen closer to his side. It was almost eleven, and the farther they walked from the brightly lit field, the darker and more silent it became.

He glanced at Jen, his chest aching at the sight of her furrowed brow and solemn expression. No doubt she was replaying the moment they'd shared hours earlier. When he'd asked to kiss her and had every intention of doing it properly. And thoroughly.

Only, he'd been too overcome by the surge of emotion welling inside him to continue. Had become focused on her eyes instead, peering deep and trying his damnedest to see if what he'd felt was reflected there. The need to know had overtaken him and the questions still hovered on the tip of his tongue.

Jen glanced up, locking eyes with him briefly before looking away.

Colt took a deep breath. He might not know which word fit these unfamiliar emotions coursing through him, but he knew for a fact which one didn't. *Friend* was no longer an accurate representation of his feelings toward Jen.

Hearing Margaret yawn, Colt looked down, smiling gently as his sister scrubbed the back of her free hand over her eyes. She'd argued hard against leaving the party.

"Yep," he said. "That's exactly why I suggested we call it a night."

Margaret blinked up at him and grinned. "All right," she grumbled good-naturedly. "I might be a little bit tired, but I'm not too tired to go to the race tomorrow."

He slowed as they reached the front porch, reluctantly releasing Margaret's hand and nudging her toward the door. "You will be if you don't get a good night's sleep, which is why you're gonna go straight to your room, brush your teeth and crawl in the bed."

"Okay." She bounded up the steps, but stopped at the door and turned. "Will you come up and say good-night?"

Colt nodded, relaxing at the thought of his new nightly routine. Tucking Margaret safely in bed and whispering good-night had become the highlight of the last two evenings. "Of course."

"G'night, Ms. Jen," Margaret called out, spinning around and opening the door.

"Good night, Meg."

Jen's gentle tone sent a fresh wave of longing through Colt, but he waited until Margaret made it inside before facing her.

"We need to talk, Jen." He tensed as she slid her arm from his and took a step back.

"About earlier?" she asked, shoving her hands in her pockets and studying the ground.

"Yeah. That and—" he glanced over his shoulder at the soft light emanating from inside the house, where Margaret was preparing for bed "—other things."

Jen rocked on her heels and lifted her head. Her brown eyes lingered on his mouth and sparked a sense of urgency within him.

"I still want to kiss you," he rasped. "And more than that. I want to—"

"Please don't," she said, rushing the words out, her fingers fumbling over his lips, stilling them. Her whisper was strained with the same desperation that filled her eyes. "Whatever it is you're about to say, once you say it, it'll always be there. It could change everything between us."

He took her hands in his and kissed her fingertips. "Things have already changed. They changed that night in that bed, and I was a fool to think we could just forget it." His gut roiled as a new possibility formed, and he pressed closer. "Have *you* been able to forget?"

She shook her head, then turned her hands over in his, squeezing his palms. "No. But I just… I can't do this right now, Colt." Her chest lifted on a deep inhalalation and she gestured over her shoulder toward the stables. "There's so much riding on tomorrow's race.

I need to focus. And Margaret's looking forward to the trip." She bit her lip, eyes pleading with his. "Please. Can we put this on hold for now? I've got to keep my head in the game."

Dread surged through him at the thought of her losing focus in the alley or while tearing around the dirt at top speed. "Okay." He forced himself to release her and move back. "It can wait."

Jen straightened, a heavy breath leaving her. "Thank you." Her slight smile vanished as soon as it appeared. "I'm going to spend some time with Diamond before turning in. We're still pulling out at seven tomorrow morning, aren't we?"

"Yeah. That'll give you plenty of time to check the place out and prepare." The tense lines beside her mouth reminded him how anxious she always became the night before a competition. "Take your time with Diamond. I'll get all the gear loaded early so you can squeeze in some extra sleep."

She nodded, eyes moving slowly over Raintree's grounds for a few moments. "It's nice here. But it's time for me to get back into the routine again." She stared ahead blankly, chin trembling. "I need this win tomorrow, Colt. It could make or break me."

His throat ached at the fear in her expression. "You're gonna do great, Red," he whispered.

Jen nodded and strolled down the winding path toward the stables. Colt watched until she disappeared from sight. He forced himself to turn on his heel and make his way inside to knock on Margaret's door.

"Meg?"

"Come in," she called.

Colt opened the door, a chuckle escaping him as Margaret, clad in pink pajamas, dashed out of the bathroom. She raced across the hardwood floor, then jumped onto the bed and snuggled under the blankets.

"All set?"

"Yep," she said, smiling widely and clutching the sheet beneath her chin.

Colt walked over and reached down, tucking the blankets around her as she giggled. "There. Snug as—"

"A bug in a rug," Margaret finished for him, laughing. She stopped giggling and blinked up at him, a shy look crossing her features. "Colt? Can I ask you something?"

He nodded. "Shoot."

"How do you know when it's the right time to kiss someone?"

*Ah, hell.* He winced, his face heating at the eager curiosity in her eyes. And it was his own fault, putting the moves on Jen like he had in front of her.

He rubbed his hands awkwardly over his jeans, then sat down on the bed, carefully collecting his thoughts. "Well. It depends."

She wiggled, pushing her way up from the blankets to a seated position. "On what?"

"On...lots of things, really." He gripped the back of his neck, kneading the knot forming there. "Like how well you know a person. Or the circumstances."

"What kind of circumstances?"

"Well..." His breath left him in a helpless exhalation. "You don't want to just jump into something like that. When you do it, it should mean something."

Colt looked down, the guilty heat in his cheeks snaking down his neck as he recalled all the random, meaningless nights he'd shared with women in the past. All the hearts he'd broken on the circuit. And all the kisses he'd wasted that, had he waited, he could've saved for Jen.

He shifted, facing Margaret. "Wait, Meg. For as long as it takes. Just wait until you meet the right person. Until you know for sure it's something you really want to do and that you're ready."

Her brow furrowed, confused frustration clouding her expression. "How will I know I'm ready?"

Colt stilled. His arms tingled as he remembered holding Jen, and his chest warmed at the thought of holding her forever.

"You'll know because it'll feel right."

He pictured Margaret years from now. Attending high school. Going to football games and parties with friends. Dealing with peer pressure. Dating. Making her first life-changing decisions.

A heavy fear lodged in his gut at the thought of his sister being alone. Without him to guide and protect her.

Colt slid his hands down her arms and squeezed. "I want you to listen hard and remember this. Don't ever let any boy talk you into kissing—or anything else—before you're ready. No boy who truly loves you will push you into anything. He'll wait, too. Because if he loves you, what he really wants to touch is your heart."

Her small teeth nibbled on her lower lip and she looked down, whispering, "But what if a boy never loves me?"

Colt sighed and smoothed a hand over her blond curls. "The right one will, Meg. Just wait till you find him."

"Do…" She glanced up, cheeks flushing. "Do you love me?"

Colt's heart stopped beating. It halted painfully right there in his chest, waiting for Margaret to smile again and give it a reason to start back up.

His throat closed and he swallowed hard before saying, "More than anything, baby girl."

Margaret smiled. "I love you, too, Colt." She threw her arms around his neck and squeezed, kissing his cheek and whispering in his ear, "I like it here. I wish we never had to leave."

That feeling returned, swelling so much in his chest he thought he'd burst. He wrapped his arms around Margaret and hugged her tight, wondering if he could manage to let her go. Questioning if he could load up, drive back to the circuit and leave Margaret behind.

If Jen won tomorrow, she'd begin mapping out the best route to hit the most competitions. She'd ask him to help her find the best opportunities to earn the highest rank in the smallest amount of time. And she'd expect him to leave first thing with her and Tammy. Just as he always had.

Unless he took Dominic up on his offer and decided to stay at Raintree.

Colt froze, unable to imagine standing still while Jen moved on without him. And even more disconcerted by the thought of her traveling on her own. Preparing for races without his encouragement and hitting the dirt without his support.

An uneasiness trickled through him. He could name it now. What he felt for Jen. It was the same thing he felt for Margaret.

*Love.* He loved Jen. As much as he loved his sister. And he was suddenly terrified that circumstances might not allow him to love and support them both.

# Chapter 10

Jen adjusted Diamond's girth strap for the fifth time, her fingers shaking so badly she could barely maintain her hold on it. She balled her hands into fists and tried to force the shaking to stop. Just as she had a thousand times since her boots had hit the dirt of the Springfield fairgrounds several hours earlier.

The hard rock blaring from the PA system increased in volume and the sounds of the crowd gathered in the outdoor arena at her back grew in tandem, scrambling her thoughts and blurring her focus. After a series of loud clicks, floodlights brightened the grounds, signaling the race would start soon.

Jen glanced to her left at the warm-up ring. Several racers were already walking or jogging their horses, performing turns and circles wherever space allowed. She should have Diamond in there already, but her nerves were too shot to start yet. And the last thing she needed was for her anxiety to pass on to Diamond.

Flashes went off by the alley gate, startling her. A line of reporters and photographers were setting up equipment and testing camera angles in order to capture just the right shots during the race. The Springfield rodeo was much bigger than Jen had anticipated. Despite being one of the smaller venues, Springfield's 1D race had enticed a high number of the best competitors, which in turn had brought out the largest crowd of spectators Jen had seen in months.

"You all right, boy?" she asked, moving a clammy palm over Diamond's broad shoulder.

He shuffled his feet and settled into a solid stance, attention on the other horses.

"You're always ready, aren't you?" She pressed her forehead to his thick neck and whispered, "We can do this."

But even to her ears the phrase sounded weak and ineffective. Her heart pounded painfully fast, making it hard to breathe. She'd gotten used to a bad case of nerves before the start of a race, but she'd never been this anxious before. And after Colt's attempt to discuss the change in their relationship last night, sitting so closely to him during the drive to Springfield had only increased her anxiety.

Colt's muscular form and handsome smile had always captured her attention. But now, something more pulled her to him. The rich tone of his voice had her longing to press her cheek to his chest. To hear his strong heartbeat and feel his words vibrate beneath his warm skin. To lie still within the safe circle of his arms and never leave.

All of which were the very last kind of thoughts she should be entertaining at the moment.

Lord, she wished Tammy could've made it to Springfield in time to compete. Or just to meet her. But her friend had texted last night to say she and Karla had already begun driving in the opposite direction for another competition. Jen had called more than once this morning just to hear Tammy's voice, but voice mail kicked in each time, which meant they were already busy preparing for a race, too.

*Just relax.* Jen inhaled, trying to calm the trembling in her fingers. *Focus.*

"Hey, Jen."

She straightened quickly, composing her features, and looked over her shoulder.

Laice Clements stood with her paint horse at her side, smiling.

Jen relaxed slightly at the sight of her friendly eyes. Laice had always been a joy to compete with. She was supportive of everyone around her, no matter how tough the competition.

"It's good to see you again," Laice said. "I got worried when I didn't come across you in Davie last weekend. I can usually count on bumping in to you there."

Jen nodded. "I couldn't make it this year. I took a week off to help Colt out."

Her friend's smile faded. "Word travels fast on the circuit. I was sorry to hear about Colt's parents. How's he doing?"

"Better." Jen gestured toward the stands surrounding the dirt arena. "He's here with his sister."

Laice's green eyes brightened. "Colt has a sister?"

"Yeah." Jen smiled, a pleasant sensation moving through her. "Her name's Margaret. She's nine."

Jen craned her neck, straining for a glimpse of Margaret's blond hair or Colt's wide shoulders in the stands. Her stomach dropped when she couldn't pinpoint them. Where were they?

She cleared her throat, scanning the crowd and adding, "Margaret's never been to a race before."

Laice laughed. "Oh, she'll love it. Once she sees you ride, she'll be begging for her own horse." Her laughter faded. "I'm really glad I ran into you. You probably don't remember, but I was competing in my first race when I met you. I was so nervous I could barely see straight, and you stood right at my side and gave me a pep talk before I hit the alley. I suppose it's fate that I'd see you again at my last one."

Jen spun back to her. "Your last one?"

"Yeah. I'm going to hang up my saddle after tonight." Laice's smile was wistful. "I've been at this for a few years now and I just don't have what it takes."

Jen started to speak, but Laice held up a hand.

"It's okay," she said, shaking her head. "I'm not above admitting it. There's only a few spots at the top, and so many of us, you know? Besides, I'm getting tired. It took me a while to realize that if you run at top speed all the time, it's just a fact that your motor's bound to break down at some point." She shrugged. "This isn't something you can do forever." Her smile returned. "I'm starting college in the fall. I've put it on hold long enough and it's time to get serious about the future."

Jen's mouth ran dry. She pried her tongue from the roof of it and asked, "What are you going to major in?"

Excitement flitted across Laice's features. "I've been thinking about medicine." She laughed. "I've had more success on the circuit helping racers with injuries than I have actually winning. So that's something I'm going to explore. But the possibilities are endless, really."

Jen forced her voice to remain steady. "Congratulations."

"Thanks." Laice dipped her head toward Diamond. "Have a safe run today. I'm pulling for you, Jen." She gathered up her horse's lead and clucked her tongue, walking toward the warm-up area.

A wave of nausea swept through Jen. She spun back to Diamond, placing her hands flat on the saddle and closing her eyes.

*I just don't have what it takes.*

She sucked in a sharp breath, recalling Laice's words and thinking about her conversation with her mom.

*You've wasted years already, and if you're not careful, you're going to use up the best ones you've got left chasing something that will never happen.*

Her mother's words cut deep, causing the violent shaking in Jen's hands to travel down her torso and invade her legs.

What would she do if she failed to come in first again? If she continued losing and didn't make it to Vegas?

Go back to Hollow Rock? Accept a dead-end job with no hope of improving her or her mother's future? Prove she was just another nobody from nowhere?

Her shoulders dropped. She'd be a bigger joke than ever in Hollow Rock. A ridiculous dreamer who had the audacity to think she could make it big. It'd prove to everyone how foolish she'd been to believe she could hold her own against talented athletes. And all the years of hard work would be exactly what her mother had predicted.

*Wasted.* She stifled a groan and hung her head, her chest aching.

"Red." Big palms settled over her hands and warm, solid strength pressed against her back.

Jen almost sagged against Colt in relief.

"You all right?" His low murmur tickled her ear. "We waited for you by the warm-up ring for over half an hour. You should be out there by now."

She lifted her head and turned, squirming beneath the weight of his stare. "I'm about to. I just…"

Her throat closed and she looked away, her eyes scanning the competitors milling around the warm-up ring. She studied the reporters and photographers lined up along the alley and the spectators laughing in the stands.

"Jen." Colt cupped a hand to her cheek. "You can do this."

The pressure in her chest eased. She nodded and pulled her shoulders back.

A sharp whistle cracked the air and they jumped, Diamond jerking his head with a snort.

Margaret skipped over, pulling two pink-stained fingers from her mouth and pumping the air with a fist. Her other hand clutched the white stick of a massive cloud of cotton candy.

"Go, Ms. Jen," she shouted.

"Hey," Colt said hastily, placing a hand on Margaret's shoulder and frowning. "Let's save that for the stands, okay? You're gonna rattle Diamond."

Jen smiled, the sight of Margaret in her pink cowboy boots and tan hat too adorable to resist. The knot between her shoulder blades untied at the excited gleam in Margaret's eyes.

"Oh, she's all right," Jen said, squatting down to brush one of Margaret's curls away from the cotton candy. "Are you having fun so far?"

"Yep." The girl nodded, her eyes darting over the arena and the warm-up ring before returning to Jen. "Colt let me watch the other racers warm up. There's lots of big horses over there and they're fast. So fast I bet I'd fly right off if I were on 'em. But you wouldn't, Ms. Jen." Her expression grew serious. "You're faster than all of them and you're going to whoop the stew out of 'em."

Jen laughed, though her stomach still churned. "That's nice of you to say. But I have my work cut out for me."

"Uh-uh." Margaret shook her head and looked up, her expression full of admiration.

"You're gonna be the best one out there." She pointed to a wrinkled poster tacked to a wooden light pole. "There's a band playing after the race. Colt said we could wait for you and dance after you cool Diamond down, if you want. And they have all kinds of stuff to eat if you get hungry later. Like boiled peanuts and popcorn and corn dogs and—"

"Cotton candy?" Jen asked, tapping the stick. "Exactly how many of these have you had tonight, hmm?"

"One." Colt eyed Margaret's furrowed brow and added, "And that's plenty."

She wrinkled her nose but grinned.

"I think that's for the best," Jen said, wiping a bit of pink fluff from the corner of Margaret's mouth. "If you eat much more of this you're gonna turn pink all over."

Margaret smiled and stuck her tongue out. "Mah tongue ith alweady pink."

Jen laughed, then caught her breath as the girl hurled herself forward, wrapping her arms around Jen's back.

"Colt said he always stays up front so you can see him when you come out," Margaret whispered, her lips warm and sticky. "We already got a place saved for us by the gate. So look for me, too, when it's your turn, okay?"

Jen hugged her back, a sweet peace settling inside her and stilling her nerves. "You'll be the first one I look for," she whispered.

"All right, Meg," Colt said, touching her shoulder. "We need to head back so Jen can warm up."

Jen stood, smiling as Margaret bit off a hunk of cotton candy and took Colt's hand.

He hesitated, his blue eyes moving over Diamond, then hovering on Jen's face. "You're gonna be great. Just stay focused and be careful out there."

"I will," she said.

Jen watched them leave. Colt moved with purposeful steps, tall and strong, while Margaret swung his hand in hers, strolling along at his side. The crowd swallowed them up.

Jen flexed her hands, turned back to Diamond and gathered up his lead. "Ready, boy?"

They spent twenty minutes warming up in the ring before moving into place at the back of the line, walking every few minutes to keep Diamond's legs supple. She shook her head as they walked past the other waiting riders. Ironic that she'd end up running last two competitions in a row. Seemed last was the only position she'd ever been guaranteed in her life.

Night had set in and the bright lights hummed overhead as she and Diamond waited their turn in the rear. A familiar rhythm took over the arena. An announcer shouted names over a continuous stream of music. The alley gate clanged open repeatedly with each racer's entrance and exit. And the shouts of the crowd rose as the line grew shorter.

"Bring her home, folks! Bring her home," the announcer yelled.

The crowd cheered the most recent racer in and the horse drew up at the gate, breathing hard as the rider slowed him to a stop, then circled back around toward the alley. A flash of light exploded as the cameras snapped and whirred.

"That's a 15.27 for Karen Thompson, which puts her in second place. Time to beat is still 14.43 and we have one more cowgirl up. Put your hands together for Jen Taylor."

Jen closed her eyes as the voice continued to blare over the speakers, her palms tightening around the reins. *14.43*. She'd never earned above a 15.12 in competitions. And that was on her best day.

The gate clanged open and she glanced up, scouring the crowd for Colt. There were so many strange faces and unfamiliar voices, the constant camera flashes and heavy beat of music only adding to the chaos.

Beads of sweat broke out on her forehead, slipping from beneath the brim of her hat and streaming down her cheeks. Diamond jerked his head and stumbled back.

*A 14.43.* There was no way—

A sharp whistle rang out to the right. Jen's eyes shot to the stands, then moved to the fence, landing on Margaret's smiling face. She stood beside Colt, holding her cotton candy with one hand and waving her hat wildly in the air with the other.

*You're gonna be the best one out there.*

Jen's hands steadied and she released a slow breath as Colt nodded. His blue eyes were warm and supportive.

She pushed her hat more firmly on her head and faced forward, eyes planted on the first pocket. "Go for great," she whispered.

Jen gave Diamond a swift kick and they blasted down the alley.

Colt tensed as Diamond tore into the arena at top speed. The horse's white mane and tail, a sharp contrast to the dirt, rippled in wild arcs as he and Jen shot toward the first barrel.

"Fire and Ice are running hot right out of

the gate," the announcer blared over the PA. "Let's see how they take this first turn…"

Margaret grabbed the top fence rail and pulled, hoisting herself up on the bottom rung.

Colt put one hand around her arm to help her balance and his other hand grabbed the top fence rail. He held his breath, his lungs burning, as Jen arrived at the first barrel, gripped the saddle horn and anchored down.

Dirt flew from beneath Diamond's hooves as the horse dug deep, carving a close curve and hugging the barrel. They rounded the turn smoothly and Jen immediately rose higher in the saddle, lifting the reins and urging Diamond on to the next.

Margaret whistled. The high-pitched sound rang in Colt's ears as she bounced against his side in excitement. "Look at her go!"

Diamond and Jen streaked across the dirt and angled in toward the next turn. A bright flash exploded just as they began curving around the second barrel, the photographer crouching on the ground aiming for the perfect shot.

"Focus, Red," Colt whispered, lifting his foot and pressing it on the lowest rung of the fence. "Stay focused."

She did, executing the second turn as flawlessly as the first. Excited cries spilled into the arena.

"Two down and on to the third," the voice blared from the PA, shouting over the stadium noise and music. "Help her out, folks. She comes out of this clean and she might have a huge check waiting for her on the other side."

"Faster, Ms. Jen," Margaret yelled, pumping her cotton candy in the air.

Colt's heart stalled as Jen and Diamond shot toward the third barrel. The fence rattled beneath the relieved jerks of his hand as she hit the mark perfectly, then sprinted toward the finish. "Go, baby," he urged.

"This could be a record setter, folks." The speakers distorted the shouted words, mixing the announcer's fast chatter with the fans' shouts. "Help this gal home!"

Jen and Diamond were a blur as they whipped across the finish line, before cutting to the side and slowing to a trot along the fence.

"Put your hands together. We might have ourselves a winner here." The speakers crackled over the noise filling the fairgrounds. "The final scores will be up in just a moment."

"She was fantastic," Margaret shouted. Her

cotton candy fell from her hand onto the grass as she clambered higher on the fence.

"Careful." Colt chuckled, steadying her.

Margaret thrust her arm out, palm in the air, as Jen and Diamond approached. "Way to go, Ms. Jen!"

Jen laughed, breathing hard. She leaned over in the saddle and high-fived Margaret. Several fans followed suit, lining up on the fence and waiting for their high fives as Jen and Diamond walked by, then circled back.

"And the score is up," the announcer bellowed, his voice pitching higher. "It's a 14.38. One of the highest scores we've had here in Springfield. Jen Taylor is your winner for the night. Keep your eye on this gal, folks. Come December, she may be leading the pack in Vegas."

The cheers grew deafening. Colt's chest swelled as Jen made her way back, her gaze locking with his. He'd never been prouder or happier for her.

She smiled, her flushed cheeks lifting and brown eyes sparkling. "Not too bad, huh?" she called out breathlessly.

"Not too bad," he shouted back.

The gate swept open, clinking and groaning on its hinges. Rapid flashes and whirring clicks erupted on both sides of the exit.

Jen glanced down, her red hair bouncing over her back. "See you in a bit."

She winked, nudged Diamond with her heels and headed toward the alley, smiling even wider as reporters called out questions and requests for interviews.

"Can I go help Ms. Jen cool Diamond down?" Margaret asked, hopping off the fence.

"Not right now, Meg." He grabbed her elbow. "Jen's going to be busy for a while doing interviews and packing up. We'll have to wait until things die down and she's able to get away."

Margaret's face fell.

"We can stand outside the cooldown area and watch, though," Colt added, taking her hand and tugging her out of the moving throng of spectators.

He reached down, scooped up the cotton candy and threw it in a nearby trash can. They paused by the alley gate, waiting for the crowd to thin out, then made their way over to Jen.

She was walking Diamond in slow lines. A group of reporters stood close by the racers, snapping pictures and shouting questions. The number of bystanders surrounding the small space made it impossible for Colt and Margaret to get through.

"I can't see," she said, rising to her tiptoes.

"There's not much to see, Meg," Colt replied.

Almost half an hour passed before Jen finished cooling Diamond down. Then the interviews started, each new round of questions lasting longer than the one before it. And photographs followed. A few with Jen posing on her own, some of her standing with fellow racers and the majority with her astride Diamond.

They waited through all of it, Margaret leaning more heavily against Colt's leg with each passing minute. She perked up a bit when the music from the band started.

"Wanna go back to the arena?" Colt asked, glancing over his shoulder at the brightly lit stage. "We could dance a time or two."

Margaret shook her head. "Not without Ms. Jen," she said quietly, wrapping her arms around his waist and pressing her cheek to his side.

Colt hugged Margaret, suddenly having no desire to return to the arena, either. Not to dance, ride a bull or for any other reason.

He watched as Jen moved farther away

with Diamond for another round of pictures. Several photographers followed, scrambling with their gear and calling out Jen's name.

Colt's stomach sank deeper with each step they took, the separation becoming more acute when Jen didn't look back or search him out in the crowd like she usually did.

He tensed, the elation he felt from Jen's win at odds with the painful knowledge that she was moving in another direction. And he found himself wishing Jen was by his side again, looking up at the stars, enjoying a cool drink and sharing a few laughs.

He'd enjoyed doing that so much at Raintree Ranch. Where time moved at a slower pace and every day was just that much sweeter. Where Margaret knew she was loved and every one of her days began and ended with him at her side. It was a place he'd never thought he'd find.

*Home.* A fullness entered Colt's chest, expanding his heart and bringing him peace. That was what Raintree had become. For him and for Margaret. What he'd helped to create for her. And he knew he could never take Margaret away from it. Or ever leave her again.

"When's she coming back?" his sister

asked. She blinked up at him, her eyes and voice heavy.

He rubbed a shaky hand over her back and decided right then that he'd do everything in his power to make sure Margaret never felt forgotten. That she would always know, without a doubt, that she was loved. And that with him, she would always come first. Whatever it might cost him.

Colt pulled her closer, drawing comfort from the press of her small frame, and tried to accept the fact that he and Jen might have to go their separate ways.

## Chapter 11

Colt palmed the steering wheel and turned slowly onto Raintree's dirt driveway. The truck bounced and swayed over several familiar dips and bumps, the trailer squeaking rhythmically as they drew closer to the main house.

His muscles relaxed and his pulse steadied, the knowledge that his feet would be on the solid ground of the ranch again soothing him.

The drive back from Springfield hadn't taken that long, because there'd been little traffic on the road. But they hadn't left the fairgrounds until hours after the race ended, and it was now after midnight. They'd waited for Jen's interviews and photo sessions to finish before loading up Diamond and packing away their gear.

"According to that reporter, I should rank fourth when the standings come out next week," Jen whispered at his side. She shifted in the passenger seat, her cell phone lighting up the truck's cab as her fingers moved over the screen.

Colt frowned and focused on navigating the winding driveway. Jen had looked up from her phone only once the entire trip back. Her attention had remained focused on her texts with Tammy and her nervous search for the results of other races in neighboring districts.

"I think he might know what he's talking about," she said, pointing a finger at the glowing screen. "I added everything up, and I've cleared forty thousand dollars this season, with tonight's winnings included in the count." She hesitated, dragging her teeth over her bottom lip. "I don't know if that's right, though. I've never been real good with numbers." Her voice lifted. "But it could be right. By the time we get back to the circuit, I might actually be ranked fourth with the pot I just won."

Unease settled in Colt's gut. He propped

his elbow on the windowsill and rubbed a hand over his jaw.

"Colt? That could be right, couldn't it?"

He glanced at her. The hope raising her dark brows and lighting her face made his chest ache. "Yeah," he whispered, managing a small smile. "That could be right."

A low rattle sounded from the back of the cab. Colt looked in the rearview mirror, catching a glimpse of Margaret huddled against the window. Her small mouth fell open and a louder round of snores began.

He smiled, turning back and meeting Jen's amused eyes before facing forward.

"She's knocked out," Jen said. She laughed softly and reached back to sweep a strand of hair away from Margaret's face. "It'll be a shame to wake her."

His smile slipped, drawing his spirits down with it.

They reached the end of the driveway and he eased the truck to a stop, then cut the engine. "I'm gonna get her in bed. Then we've got to talk, Jen."

Her smile disappeared, too. But she nodded, unbuckling her seat belt and lifting her hip to slide her phone into her pocket. "Okay.

I'll get Diamond settled, then wait for you in your room."

Colt took his time getting Margaret tucked in for the night, walking her into the house and standing by her side as she brushed her teeth, her eyes drowsy.

"In you get," he said, helping her into bed and tucking the covers around her shoulders.

"G'night, Colt," she murmured.

A sleepy smile crossed her face as he kissed her forehead, her eyelids fluttering shut.

"Good night, Meg," he whispered.

He stayed there for a while, closing his eyes and leaning against the doorjamb, before making his way to the guest wing. His legs grew heavier with each step.

Jen was waiting inside for him. She stood at the window, her back to him as she stared out into the dark night.

"You're not returning to the circuit with me, are you?"

Colt drew to a halt in the middle of the room, his heart tripping painfully at the sadness in her low voice.

He pried his tongue from the roof of his dry mouth and answered, "No."

Her shoulders slumped and she lowered her head, her red hair rippling across her back.

He forced himself to continue. "I've decided to take Dominic up on his offer. It'll give me a chance to slow down. Put down roots." He inhaled, his lungs stalling. "I'm going to buy some land from him and build a house on one of the back lots."

"For you and Meg?" Jen pushed her hands into her front pockets, drawing further into herself. "You're going to keep her?"

Colt nodded, knowing she couldn't see him, but aware she didn't need to. "I'm calling Jack first thing in the morning. I'm gonna tell him to send me the guardianship papers and let my grandmother know I'm keeping Meg." His chest tightened at Jen's silence. "I won't leave her. She's my sister. My family." He held the word on his tongue, savoring the soothing feel of it and weighing it against the knot in his gut. "You've got to understand—"

"I do," she choked out. She spun to face him, her smile weak and chin trembling. "I do understand. I just wish…" Her brave expression collapsed and she turned her head to the side, a tear streaking down her cheek.

He strode swiftly across the room and wrapped his arms around her. She shook in his embrace, the entire length of her body trembling against his own. He held her silently for several minutes, sliding his hands over her back and lowering his lips to kiss the top of her head.

"There's something else I need to say." Colt breathed her in, closing his eyes at the sweet scent of her hair and relishing the rapid pounding of her heart against his own. "I love you, Jen." He clutched her closer and raised his head, meeting her eyes as she looked up at him. "I love everything about you."

Her mouth parted on a swift breath and he slowly traced the outline of her lips with a fingertip.

"I love how brave you are, regardless of what you're up against. I love how gentle and patient you are with Meg. How generous, kind and forgiving you are with everyone, including me." A low laugh escaped him. "I even love the way you brushed me off when we first met." He sobered, his hands moving to cradle her face. "How you've expected more of me. And how you've made me into a better man."

Her breasts lifted against him as she took a deep breath, her hands leaving her pockets and curling against his chest.

He touched his mouth to hers, parting her lips with his and whispering again, "I love you and I don't want you to leave."

With a soft cry, she slid her hands up his chest and wrapped them around the nape of his neck, kissing him back.

The sweet taste of her touched his tongue and the gentle press of her body against his heated his blood, urging him to delve deeper into the kiss and move his hands over her curves with greater purpose.

He lifted his head and nudged her chin up with a knuckle until she met his gaze again. "Do you love me?"

"Yes," she whispered.

His chest warmed at her words but his heart tripped at the dismay in her expression. "Then stay with me, Red. Marry me."

She squeezed her eyes shut and tugged his mouth back down to hers, her kiss almost desperate as it silenced him.

He let her take over for a few moments, relishing the passionate movements of her body and hands as she explored him. And he became more anxious than ever to hear the words he hoped for spilling from her lips.

"Stay," he urged, lowering himself to his knees and tugging her shirt from her jeans. "Be my wife. We'll build a home of our own. Start a family."

Her belly rippled, quivers chasing across

the flat expanse of her creamy skin and he gave in to the overwhelming urge to nuzzle his face against it. Imagining the possibility of a child nestled safely there one day. His and Jen's. Protected and loved.

He pressed his lips to the smooth skin above her belly button and hugged her legs, his callused palms moving over the denim covering the toned muscles of her thighs.

"Colt." She looked down at him with dark eyes, her fiery curls spilling over her shoulders. Her fingers cradled his head gently, her mouth moving, but no sound emerging.

He was afraid to let go of her. Because if he did, he knew he may never be able to hold her again.

He flexed his arms around her, getting a solid grip on her hips and hoisting her up. He carried her over to the bed, laid her down gently, then lowered his body onto hers. "You want me to stop?" he asked, smoothing her hair from her face and waiting.

She shook her head and rose to kiss him again.

Logic left him, the strength of emotion that blazed in his chest drove his hands to remove her clothing. To caress and cherish every inch of her. He lingered over her breasts and the curves of her hips, pausing briefly to help her remove his own clothing, then moved to his back and savored her gentle advances.

At the sight of her flushed cheeks, kiss-reddened lips and yearning eyes, he rolled over her to seek her warmth.

Her arms and legs parted, her fingertips sweeping over his back and her heels hooking around his thighs. She opened to him completely, welcoming him. Urging him on as he entered her slowly, moving with the rhythm of their shared breaths.

Colt held her gaze as soft cries escaped her and the increasing intensity of pleasure swept over her face.

She came apart in his arms and he followed, holding himself still above her. He knew what the answer would be. Had known all along. But he had to ask one more time. "Stay with me."

Jen squeezed her eyes shut and tears seeped from the corners, gliding slowly across her temples and disappearing into her hair.

Colt flinched, an unbearable pain piercing through the pleasure that still throbbed so strongly in his veins. Her mouth barely moved, but he heard the fractured words just the same.

"I can't."

* * *

Jen shivered as Colt disentangled himself from her and left the bed. Her skin, which had flamed under his touch minutes ago, turned ice-cold, and the chill cut through her all the way to her bones. She'd tried so hard not to hurt him. Had tried to say goodbye the best way she could. But she'd failed at both.

She dragged the sheet over her breasts and sat up, her stomach churning as he jerked his jeans on. "I'm sorry, Colt."

He didn't answer. The rasp of his zipper closing and the clang of his belt buckling filled the room.

"Colt?" Jen wrapped the sheet around her and stood, pressing her palm to the warm skin of his broad back.

He turned, capturing her hand and squeezing it in his, his eyes peering down at her. "Do you want to marry me?"

*Yes.* Jen bit back the word, stilling her tongue. She ached to say it. To tell him. But if she did, she wouldn't have the strength to walk away.

"Because if you do, I'll wait," he said. "I'll figure out a way to keep Margaret with us until you win at Vegas. Then afterward, we can all come back and settle at Raintree."

She shook her head, forcing sound from her constricted throat. "It's not that simple, Colt. I can't just quit after Vegas. There are so many other things to consider."

He stilled. "What things?"

She slid her hand from his, holding the sheet at her chest to keep from reaching for him. "Tammy, for one. I can't leave her on her own out there. She—"

"Tammy's a grown woman. And a strong one at that," Colt said. "She knows the road and has plenty of connections. She'd be fine without either one of us. Has been since we left the circuit."

"Maybe. But I promised her I'd come back."

"What else?" he asked quietly. "Tell me what else there is to consider, Jen."

She moved closer, wincing at the pain in his expression. "I'm so close to winning. Closer than I've ever been. And even if I do win, I can't just hang up my saddle and walk away. It's part of me. It's what I do. The only thing I've ever been good at. I've worked too hard for too long to give it all up. I've sacrificed so much…" She straightened, steadying her voice. "I can't throw it all away. I have to keep going. No matter what."

"No matter what?" Colt stepped back, his

face paling. "I used to know someone who lived by that mantra."

A wave of nausea swept over Jen. "I'm not like your father, Colt. And neither are you."

"I used to think I wasn't," he said. "But I did exactly what he would've done, initially, had he been in my position. I decided right off that I wasn't going to take Meg. That I was just going to leave her in the care of strangers and go on my way. Leave her like I did every other female that crossed my path." He grimaced. "Like I tried to leave you a couple of weeks ago in that bar."

"But you changed your mind. You've chosen to be honest with me." Jen's voice broke. "And you're staying with Margaret now."

"Yeah. I am." He tilted his head, his eyes thoughtful as they roved over her face. "Who did you call that night in the hayloft? When you said you were touching base with home?"

She ducked her head, her cheeks flaming.

"Who was it?" he prompted. "Jen?"

"My mom."

Colt nodded slowly. "You've never talked about her. Not in all the time we've known each other. I only recall two times over the years that you left to go home, and both times, you were back on the circuit within three days." He looked away. "I can't really fault you for that, since I did the same thing. But now I know what it feels like to be on the other end of it."

Jen's eyes blurred and she blinked rapidly in an attempt to clear them. "You and I both know what has to be sacrificed in order to make it out there. There's too much at stake for me to walk away. This is my chance. My shot at making something of myself. A shot at being someone who matters."

"You matter to me," Colt said softly. "And Meg."

"I know. I love you and Margaret. But I need more than that."

"Can you understand that Meg and I need more, too?" His eyes turned sad. "I'm proud of you, Jen. I know what's waiting for you out there and there's no limit to how high you could climb. But I don't think racing makes you happy anymore. Not really. No matter how much you win, the fans will stop cheering when the fun ends and they'll leave when the competition is over like always. My father valued his career more than anything else. He made enough money to build a mansion that could hold ten families but it's remained empty in every way that matters." He shook his head. "Meg has been unseen, unheard and unloved for the majority of her childhood. I know how much that hurts. And I won't ever let that happen again. With me, Meg will always know she's loved." He stepped closer. "And so would you."

Jen looked down and curled her toes underneath the fall of the sheet, unable to face him. "I know it sounds selfish and I know I'm hurting you. And that I'll hurt Margaret..." She choked back a sob, ignoring the hot wetness coursing down her cheeks. "That's the very last thing I'd ever want to do. But I can't give up racing. I need it. I need to prove that I can make it and that I can stay on top."

The warmth of his palms cupped her jaw and his thumbs drifted over her cheeks. "Who are you trying to prove this to?" he whispered.

She looked up then. "Everyone. People back home. The ones on the circuit."

Colt frowned, sweeping a blunt fingertip beneath her eyes and wiping away a fresh stream of tears. "I don't think that's what you're looking for, Red. But if it really is, is what all those other people think that important?" He paused, tipping up her chin. "More important than what I think? Or Meg? Because to us, the woman who rides into that arena is the same one riding out of it. And win or lose, we still love you just as much as we did before."

A choked cry escaped her and she hid her face against his broad chest, laying her cheek against his warm skin and absorbing the scent of him. The feel of him.

"I have to do this," she whispered.

He exhaled, his heavy breath ruffling her hair. His arms wrapped around her, holding her loosely, his callused palms moving over the bare skin of her back above the sheet.

She pressed closer, her chest squeezing to the point of pain. "I can come back and stay for a while. Once this season's over."

His chest vibrated beneath her cheek. "And what happens when the next one starts? When the next opportunity arrives?"

She closed her eyes and didn't answer.

Colt released her and moved away. He collected his shirt and boots from the floor, then paused at the door. "It's not just me anymore. I have to consider what's best for Meg. Time is the most valuable asset I have and I'm not wasting any more of it. I'm staying here with Meg and I'm going to make sure she knows that my family is what's most important in my life. Meg deserves to be remembered and loved all the time. Not just when it's convenient." His voice firmed. "And so do I."

"Colt, please—"

"I assume you and Tammy have already lined up another competition."

Jen nodded, tremors tearing through her. "Texas."

"I'll check the truck and trailer over. Pack some fresh supplies." He turned to leave. "It'll be ready for you by tomorrow morning."

Jen followed, stumbling over the sheet trailing across the floor. "I can't take your truck."

"Why not? I'll just get a new one." He stopped and looked over his shoulder, his tone resigned. "Money's not what I'm short on."

Jen stood there long after he left, staring at the empty doorway.

Eventually, she headed to the room she shared with Margaret and hesitated by the girl's bed. A couple strands of blond hair had fallen forward and settled over her mouth. They lifted gently with each soft snore.

Heart clenching, Jen reached down and carefully pushed the hair back from Meg's face, then kissed her temple.

A fresh surge of tears streamed down her cheeks and she stepped away quickly, crawled into bed and closed her eyes. Sleep eluded her, though, and she gave up as the first tendrils of morning light crept between the closed blinds. Getting up, she began packing quietly.

Afterward, Jen loaded Diamond in the trailer. She said her goodbyes to the Slade family, hugged both sets of twins and baby Ethan, then stood outside by the truck, watching as Colt made one last inspection of the vehicle.

"Everything looks good," he said, rounding the back and stopping at the driver's side door. His eyes were heavy and the shadows beneath them had darkened. "I filled the tank so you'll have plenty of gas. And I double-checked the air pressure on the tires, so they're full, too."

Jen's breath caught at the gruff sound of his voice and she managed a strained whisper. "Thank you."

"Ms. Jen?"

She turned to find Margaret standing beside the trailer. The girl wore her hat and one of her new outfits, her pink boots dusty and well broken in. She smiled, but her eyes were red-rimmed and her cheeks flushed.

A streak of pain traveled through Jen. "Hey." She knelt and held her arms out, her palms aching to pull Margaret close.

Margaret ran across the dirt and hurled herself into Jen's embrace.

Jen held her and kissed the top of her head, focusing on the green field. The image blurred in front of her. "I'm going to miss you, Meg."

"I'll miss you, too." Her thin voice shook and her shoulders jerked. "Colt said we're staying here, you know? For good."

Jen nodded, biting her lip. "I know. I bet you were glad to hear that."

"Yeah. I like it here." Margaret stepped back and dragged her hand over her tear-streaked cheeks. "So that's where we'll be," she said, her expression earnest. "If you want to come see us. We'll be here. You are going to visit soon, aren't you?"

"Of course," Jen whispered.

"Meg." Colt's big hand squeezed his sister's shoulder and he gestured toward the trailer. "Go say goodbye to Diamond. Jen has to hit the road."

Margaret nodded and left, walking back to the trailer and climbing up on the wheel to pet Diamond through the slats.

Colt cupped Jen's elbow and pulled her to her feet. "Don't make her promises you have no intention of keeping."

"I do plan to visit," she said, wrapping her hands around his biceps. "As soon as I finish the season. And I'll call—"

"Let's not do this. You have a long drive ahead of you and…" Colt's voice trailed away. His throat moved with a hard swallow and he pulled her close, wrapping his arms around her and squeezing.

Jen slid her arms up and gripped his nape, kissing his neck and breathing in the scent of his skin, memorizing as many details as she could.

"You're breaking my heart, Red," he said in a choked whisper. "But, damned if I don't still love you."

A chill swept over her and she rose on her toes, grabbing on to him and holding tight. "Colt—"

"Go." He tugged her arms from him and spun on his heel, pausing to help Margaret down from the trailer, then taking her hand and leading her away.

Jen watched them leave, forcing a smile as Margaret glanced back at her several times. It faltered, though, once they climbed the porch steps and disappeared inside the house. And she needed every bit of strength she had left to climb into the truck, crank the engine and drive away.

## *Chapter 12*

"Next up, we've got a gal from Spokane, Washington. Let's give her a strong, Southern welcome, folks."

Jen centered her seat and ran her fingers through Diamond's mane, watching as the alley gate opened and the next competitor took her position under the bright lights.

The noise inside the arena increased as the brunette kicked her horse's flanks and charged across the dirt. The Priceville, Alabama, crowd was smaller than most, but what they lacked in numbers they made up for in enthusiasm. And in winnings. An additional six thousand dollars had just been added to the pot over the last few days and the resulting payout was big by anyone's standards.

"Only six more and you're up."

Jen glanced down to her left, smiling at Tammy's excited expression. They'd both performed well over the two weeks since Jen had left Raintree, placing in all three of the competitions they'd entered. Tammy had clocked one of her best runs yet, scoring well enough to secure a position in tonight's top five. And Karla had joined up with them at each competition, holding her own with the more experienced riders.

"A 15.12 is the highest so far," Tammy continued, patting Diamond's shoulder and smiling. "Don't think you'll have a problem cracking that."

Jen shrugged. "Maybe. But only one person can get that top spot."

Tammy shook her head, stepping closer and rubbing Diamond's neck. "I don't mind coming in second as long as first goes to you," she said. "And even if you don't get first, you won't be far behind. You certainly won't be last."

Jen's smile slipped as she turned the word over in her mind, surprised to find it had lost its sting. "I don't mind being last," she said.

And for the first time, she really meant it.

She turned back to the gate, searching the stands and scanning the fence by the alley. Her stomach dropped at the sight of so many strangers' faces and the absence of two people in particular. Just as it had at each competition over the past two weeks.

Jen moved her hand across her front pocket, tracing the outline of her cell phone. "You mind watching Diamond for a minute?" she asked, swinging her leg over and hopping down.

"Sure," Tammy said, wariness crossing her features as she took the reins. "But what're you doing? You'll be up soon."

"I know," she said over her shoulder, tugging her phone from her pocket and walking away. "I just need to make a quick call."

"Don't be long," Tammy called out. "You'll miss your spot."

Jen nodded, waving away the concern and dialing. She stood outside the warm-up area, watching racers turning and loping from one end to the other. The warm night air caressed her cheeks and whispered across the phone. Her heart fluttered as she counted the rings.

"Hello?"

Jen blinked and cleared her throat, expecting the deep tone of Colt's voice, but hearing the high-pitched lilt of Margaret's.

"Hey, Meg." Her chest warmed at the sound of Margaret's excited gasp.

"Hey, Ms. Jen," she said, almost breathlessly. "Are you in Alabama already?"

Jen smiled. She'd called Colt almost every night since leaving Raintree. He'd answered every time, asking how she was doing and filling her in on Margaret's activities at school, before handing the phone to his sister.

Jen's smile slipped at the thought of the last couple calls. Colt's voice had sounded heavier each time he'd answered, his responses growing shorter with each conversation.

"Yeah." Jen forced a bright note into her tone. "We made it to Priceville last night and scoped out the arena this morning."

"Are there lots of racers at this one?"

"Quite a few." Jen watched the movements of the horses nearby, an ache blooming in her chest. "How are things your way? Did you and the boys play basketball at school again today?"

"Yep. And I beat 'em."

"All of them?" Jen teased.

"Every one of 'em. Kayden and Jayden made almost as many baskets as I did, but not enough to win. I whopped 'em good." Margaret laughed, the joyful sound ringing clear over the line. "Colt said he's gonna get us our own basketball hoop and put it up this weekend so we can practice. He said he'd show me some moves so that I'll be ready to try out for the basketball team when I get to middle school if I want to. Do you think I could make the team if I practice real hard?"

"You can do anything you put your mind to, Meg," Jen said, stilling as the phrase echoed over the line. "Anything at all."

"We all had good grades on our report cards and Mr. Logan said we can have another movie night to celebrate. I can let you know when it is ahead of time. Then maybe you could come back for that?" Margaret hesitated. "Are..." Her voice stalled, the bright cheer in it dimming. "Are you going to visit soon? 'Cause I miss you."

Jen winced at the sadness in Margaret's tone. "I—"

The sound of muffled movements came across the line and she heard Colt's voice in the background. There was silence for several moments, then the line was clear again.

"Jen."

Jen closed her eyes, wishing she could see

his face. "Hey." She dragged her teeth over her bottom lip. "How...how are you?"

"Fine." His tone was short, the word clipped. "You and Tammy make it to Priceville okay?"

"Yeah. We're at the race now. My run's almost up."

A heavy sigh sounded and Colt's voice lowered. "You can't keep doing this, Jen."

"Doing what?"

"Calling like this. Talking to Meg every night and promising to visit. She does okay until she hears your voice. Then she cries when she gets off the phone."

"I'm sorry," Jen said, heat engulfing her face and her limbs turning heavy. "I never meant to upset her. I just miss her. And you. I miss you, too, Colt." Her voice grew weak and she whispered, "So much."

He remained silent for a while, then said, "I can't do this anymore. I can't be here for Meg one hundred percent and worry about you out there at the same time. Every damned morning I wake up wondering where you're headed next and if you made it there okay. I wonder if you had a safe run or if you—" His voice broke and there was a scuffling sound before he said heavily, "You've got to let me let you go, Red."

Jen fought to draw a breath, clutching the phone closer to her ear. "If that's really what you want." She had to force out the words.

"It's not what I want," he said. "But it's what I have to do."

The announcer's voice crackled over the speakers, calling up the next competitor.

"Sounds like you need to go," Colt said. "Red?"

She stifled a sob, biting her lip until the metallic taste of blood touched her tongue. "Yeah?"

"Good luck. And be careful out there."

"I always am," she whispered.

But the line had been cut and her answer hovered on dead air.

"Jen?"

She lowered the phone to her side and looked over her shoulder. Tammy stood near the gate, holding Diamond's reins in one hand and beckoning frantically with the other.

Jen made her way over slowly, avoiding her friend's eyes as she took the reins from her.

"It's almost time," Tammy said, glancing anxiously at the line of racers surrounding them. "You're about to lose your spot."

Jen hooked her heel in the stirrup and lifted herself up, straddling Diamond and settling in. The shouts from the arena grew louder as a racer exited through the alley gate and the rider in front of Jen lined up.

"How are Colt and Margaret?"

Jen glanced at Tammy. "Okay, I guess," she said.

She turned away and gripped the saddle horn to still the shaking in her hand, recalling the strained tones of Colt's voice and the sadness underlying Margaret's.

A tremor tore through her and she flexed her fingers, realizing this was the first time she'd had a case of nerves since leaving Raintree.

"Jen?" Tammy tugged at her pant leg and peered up at her, asking softly, "Where's your head at, girl?"

Jen stilled, but didn't give her usual reply. She couldn't. Her head wasn't in the game. She wasn't focused on the winning time or the barrel pattern. And she'd given no thought to the outcome of the race.

Because it didn't matter...

Jen sagged in the saddle, the tension leaving her limbs in a peaceful rush and the trembling in her hands subsiding. It no longer mattered whether she won or lost. It didn't matter if her name was on the board or if the crowd applauded for her. Or if everyone saw her come in first.

*You can do anything you put your mind to...*

She no longer felt the need to prove anything to anyone. Including herself. She knew she could do it. She knew Diamond could, too. Heck, they'd already done it. More times than not lately. And she finally believed it deep inside. Believed it to the point that coming in first in the arena no longer mattered.

What mattered most was putting Colt and Margaret first. That they knew her, flaws and all, and still loved her. Just as she was. With or without a title. Because who she was what was important to them, not what she could do.

*I've been proud of you every day of your life.*

Her mother's words returned, filling her heart to the point it overflowed, escaping from her eyes and trickling down her cheeks.

She'd spent so much time trying to earn approval from strangers instead of spending it with those she loved. And no amount of money or success could replace the joy she'd felt when loving and supporting Colt and Margaret.

"Where's your head, Jen?" Tammy repeated, reaching up to squeeze her knee.

Jen wiped away a tear and whispered, "Don't you mean where's my heart?"

Her friend smiled. "With Colt and Margaret?"

Jen nodded and tilted her head back, looking up at the night sky. The stars here were drowned out by the floodlights. She recalled how bright the moon was at Raintree. How green the fields were and how the fun continued well past the last ray of sunshine each day.

She smiled at the thought of juice boxes and kites. Children, outdoor movies and kisses in pickup trucks. So many beautiful babies and happy kids safely at play. The ranch is a perfect place to make a home and start a family. A family with Colt and Margaret. Something worth more than any number of gold buckles. And something she wanted more than anything.

Her heart skipped a beat and she straightened, tugging on Diamond's reins and stepping out of line. "I want to go back to Raintree."

Tammy nodded. "I kind of expected that. You haven't been the same since you came back. I guess I was being selfish trying to keep you to myself."

"Come with me," Jen urged, swinging her leg over the saddle and hopping down.

Tammy shook her head, glancing toward the arena as the announcer called the next contestant. "My ride's not done here. I want a title and Karla needs a buddy for the road, so it'll work out well." She smiled through the sadness in her eyes, stepping forward and hugging her. "I want you to be happy. Don't worry about me. Just be careful going back." Her laugh ruffled Jen's hair. "Make an honest man of my cousin and don't forget that you've already got a maid of honor lined up. I'll be expecting a call once you set the date."

Jen squeezed her close once more and stepped back, wiping away a tear. "You got it. And I'll be calling you before then. A lot."

They said one last goodbye, then Jen led Diamond through his cooldown, removed his tack and loaded him in the trailer. She paused on the way to the driver's seat, walked back to the trailer and reached through the slats to give Diamond one more pat.

"Can you handle a few extra miles, boy?" Jen smiled, mentally plotting the fastest route from Alabama to Georgia. "Because there's one more stop I'd like to make before we head to Raintree."

\* \* \*

Colt shielded his eyes against the Sunday afternoon sun and called out, "Good job, Meg. Stay centered and slow it down a bit."

"Like this?"

"That's right," Colt said, watching as she realigned herself in the saddle and tapped Destiny's flanks, urging her farther out into one of Raintree's fields.

The slow gait lasted all of thirty seconds before Margaret tapped Destiny again and quickened the pace, catching up with Kayden and Jayden, who rode their horses several feet ahead of her.

"She's getting good," Dominic said at his side.

"Yeah." Colt shoved his hands into his front pockets and leaned back against the fence. "Too good. She's been begging for barrel racing lessons a lot lately."

"Yep. She's asked me, too." Dominic propped his elbows on the top fence rail and looked to his left, studying the bulls roaming in a pasture on the far side of the grounds. "Of course, I wouldn't know where to start with something like that. Bulls are more my thing."

Colt nodded, glancing at the animals he and Dominic had purchased and doing his best to keep his thoughts from straying to Jen. Just as they had every day since she'd left Raintree.

In actuality, he shouldn't have had time to think about her over the past two weeks. He'd been so busy helping Margaret with homework, riding lessons and settling in permanently at the ranch that his afternoons and evenings were full. And during the day, while Margaret attended school, he spent whatever free time he had planning and implementing the first stages of his and Dominic's new business venture, and pitching in with the daily chores.

He'd thrown himself into work purposefully, hoping the long hours and tedious tasks would keep him from thinking about Jen. Keep him from picturing her bright smile and sexy laugh. Help him avoid remembering how her gentle touch had made his skin tingle and his body hum. Maybe put an end to the way his heart bled every time he faced getting through another day without her.

Only, none of it had worked. He still missed her like hell. Still woke every morning thinking of her. Dreamed about her every night when he closed his eyes. And saying a final goodbye to her last night over the phone had been the hardest thing he'd ever had to do.

He flinched at the pain lashing through him. He'd lost so much more than a friend.

"...could hire someone."

Colt blinked, forcing his thoughts to subside and turning back to Dominic. "What?"

"I said we could hire someone. To give Meg lessons."

Colt nodded absently, a small smile fighting its way to his lips at the sight of Margaret nudging Destiny into a trot behind the boys, following them to the other end of the field. Her blond curls bounced against her back and she sat taller in the saddle than she ever had before. Her confidence had grown so much over the past weeks at Raintree and he had no doubt that he'd made the right decision to keep her here permanently.

He hadn't completely cut off Margaret's access to their father's estate, though. He'd retained ownership and would sign over his share in John W. Mead's company to Margaret in a few years. That way, she could choose which path to take when she came of age. And he'd support her decision.

Colt sighed. He just wished the path he'd chosen for himself was the one Jen wanted, too.

"Who knows?" Dominic shrugged. "If whoever we hire to give Meg racing lessons does a good job, we could consider keeping them on permanently. Maybe even make them a partner. Expand the riding clinics to include barrel racing lessons, too."

Something in Dominic's tone was off. Colt looked at him, studying the amused lift of his brow and knowing gleam in his eye.

"What's going on?" Colt asked, frowning.

Dominic adopted a bland expression. "What do you mean?"

"Don't ask me that like you don't know what I'm talking about." Colt pulled his hands from his pockets and shoved himself off the fence. "Something's up. I can tell."

Dominic's mouth twitched and he waved a hand in the air, turning away. "Just tossing ideas around, that's all."

"The hell you say—"

"Hey, Mr. Colt," Jayden shouted, galloping up the center of the field and pointing behind him. "Ms. Jen and Diamond are coming!"

Colt's eyes snapped to the driveway, scanning the empty dirt road. There was no familiar growl from his truck and no white trailer clearing the hill.

He jerked back to face Dominic, looking for some sign that what Jayden said was true.

A broad smile spread slowly across Dominic's face. "Well, hell," he drawled. "Guess we won't have to look too far to find the right person for the job."

A distant thundering of hooves erupted. Colt spun back around, his heart stumbling in his chest as a flash of red and white emerged over the hill.

Diamond galloped along the narrow strip of grass between the fence and the dirt road. Jen sat high on his back, leaning forward and moving rhythmically with each of his powerful strides. Her hair arced behind her in a fiery wave.

Excited cries erupted from the field. Kayden and Margaret trotted along the fence, doing their best to keep time with Jen. They couldn't keep up and fell farther and farther behind, but it did nothing to dampen their spirits. If anything, their whoops and cheers grew louder.

"Go, Ms. Jen," Margaret hollered, her jubilant cry echoing across the grounds.

Colt moved quickly, striding to the pasture gate and tugging it open as Jen slowed to a halt in front of it. He looked up at her, his breath catching at the rosy flush of her cheeks and the flirtatious spark in her brown eyes. Her full breasts rose and fell with her rapid breaths and her lush mouth parted enticingly as she stared down at him, almost causing his knees to buckle.

He forced himself to speak and picked out the only coherent words he could manage, stringing them into a gruff question. "Where's my truck?"

Her smile widened and she nodded toward the hill just as the pickup came barreling into view. The engine's racy roar and the clang of the trailer bouncing over potholes filled the air. Dust flew up from the tires as it sped down the drive, then screeched to an awkward halt.

"Diamond got restless a mile or so back and wanted to stretch his legs," Jen said, swinging herself to the ground. "So I saddled him up and rode him in."

Colt rubbed his hands over his jeans, gripping the denim to keep from crushing her to him. He glanced back at the dust cloud settling around his truck. "Yeah, but who…"

The driver's door creaked open and a tall woman with red hair jumped out. She slammed it shut and crossed to the front of the truck, patting the hood and chuckling.

"Woo," she gasped. "I've never driven a rig as racy as this. It's a nice ride, Jen."

Jen laughed, her warm eyes returning to his. "My mom. She likes to ride fast, too." She flushed a deeper shade of red and released Diamond's reins, allowing him to amble into the field. "I stopped by to see her on the way back and talked her into coming with me for a vacation. I thought I'd let her check out the ranch. See the sights. I called ahead and asked Dominic to reserve a room for her."

"You did?"

Now it made sense. Colt glanced over his shoulder at his friend, his own mouth quirking when Dominic ducked his head and walked over to the kids, helping them down from their saddles. The boys ran up, hugged Jen quickly, then shot over to the truck, cornering her mother and firing off questions.

Jen knelt as Margaret rushed toward her, catching her in her arms and pressing kisses to her cheeks.

Colt's chest warmed at the happiness in Jen's eyes and smile.

"You came back," Margaret said, bouncing in Jen's arms. "I'm so glad you came back."

"Me, too," she murmured, sitting back on her heels. "That's my mom over there. Ms. Nora. Why don't you go over and say hi with the boys? I've told her a lot about you and she's anxious to meet you."

Margaret smiled and nodded, then darted over to join the twins. Kayden stood on one side of Nora and Jayden on the other. Both boys had their hands propped on their hips.

Kayden's authoritative voice carried over to the field. "So how good are you at fort building?"

"Oh, Lord," Dominic rumbled, easing past Colt and Jen and striding across the driveway toward the boys. "Better head this off at the pass."

Colt and Jen shared a laugh.

Jen's laughter faded and she sobered, her shoulders lifting briefly. "My mom and I haven't always had the best relationship. A lot of that was my fault. I've been judging us both too harshly. I thought spending some time together at Raintree might help us grow closer. I was hoping, maybe, after my mom saw the place, she might decide to relocate."

Colt studied the hesitant movements of her mouth and the slight shake in her hand as she tucked a strand of hair behind her ear. His belly flipped over at her shy expression and he tried to tone down the hopeful note in his voice as he asked, "And why would she want to do that?"

Jen stepped closer, placing a palm on his chest. "Because I plan to stay."

He pulled in a deep breath and placed his hand over hers, squeezing it.

"It's simple, you see?" Jen hooked her thumb over the back of his hand, rubbing his knuckles. "There's this man I can't stop thinking about." Her voice lowered to a whisper. "He's patient and kind. He's a good listener and very considerate. And he's the best friend anyone could ask for." She paused and cleared her throat. "Only, there's this one problem."

Colt bit his lip. "What kind of problem?"

Jen smiled and placed her other hand on his chest. "I fell in love with him. He makes me happier than I've ever been. And now I want to be more than just a friend. I want to be his wife. I want to share my life with him. Every second of it. I want to wake up with him every morning and lie down beside him every night. And I want to start a family with him." Her gaze dropped to his mouth. "That is, if the offer still stands?"

Colt pulled his free hand from his pocket and cupped her face with his palm. "It does."

A shaky breath escaped her and he tugged

her closer, lowering his head and covering her mouth with his. Her lips parted, her sweet taste and her light scent heating his blood.

Conspiratorial whispers turned into a chorus of children's voices. "Mr. Colt and Ms. Jen sitting in a tree. *K-i-s-s-i—*"

Colt groaned, lifted his head and spun around, chasing them with playful smacks to their backsides as they scattered. "Get your little tails outta here."

The boys guffawed. Margaret blushed. And Dominic and Nora chuckled as they rounded the children up and herded them toward the house in the distance.

Colt laughed and shook his head, returning to Jen and rubbing his hands up and down her bare arms. "Now, where were we?"

"You were about to tell me you love me," she said.

He pulled her close again, wrapping his arms around her and pressing her against him. "I love you, Red."

"I love you, too. Now kiss me like you mean it," she teased.

Colt laughed and kissed her properly this time, his tongue slipping between her lips and his hands kneading her back. He angled deeper, savoring her soft moans of pleasure.

He raised his head briefly, his skin tingling under the desperate caress of her hands as they moved over his shoulders, and his chest warmed at her dazed expression. *Beautiful.*

"We better set the wedding date early." She smiled up at him. "Because I'm already eager to start the honeymoon."

Colt chuckled, his whole body humming with happiness. "You haven't seen me at my best yet, baby."

Jen's smile gentled. She glanced over her shoulder at the main house, which Margaret had entered, then looked back, running her eyes over his face and whispering, "Yes, I have."

Colt kissed her again and knew, without a doubt, that he'd finally come home.

\* \* \* \* \*

# Get 4 FREE REWARDS!

**We'll send you 2 FREE Books plus 2 FREE Mystery Gifts.**

FREE
Value Over
**$20**

Both the **Harlequin® Historical** and **Harlequin® Romance** series feature compelling novels filled with emotion and simmering romance.

**YES!** Please send me 2 FREE novels from the Harlequin Historical or Harlequin Romance series and my 2 FREE gifts (gifts are worth about $10 retail). After receiving them, if I don't wish to receive any more books, I can return the shipping statement marked "cancel." If I don't cancel, I will receive 6 brand-new Harlequin Historical books every month and be billed just $5.69 each in the U.S. or $6.24 each in Canada, a savings of at least 12% off the cover price or 4 brand-new Harlequin Romance Larger-Print every month and be billed just $5.59 each in the U.S. or $5.74 each in Canada, a savings of at least 14% off the cover price. It's quite a bargain! Shipping and handling is just 50¢ per book in the U.S. and $1.25 per book in Canada.* I understand that accepting the 2 free books and gifts places me under no obligation to buy anything. I can always return a shipment and cancel at any time. The free books and gifts are mine to keep no matter what I decide.

Choose one: ☐ **Harlequin Historical**
(246/349 HDN GNPD)

☐ **Harlequin Romance Larger-Print**
(119/319 HDN GNQD)

Name (please print)

Address                                                                                                          Apt. #

City                                              State/Province                                   Zip/Postal Code

**Email:** Please check this box ☐ if you would like to receive newsletters and promotional emails from Harlequin Enterprises ULC and its affiliates. You can unsubscribe anytime.

### Mail to the **Harlequin Reader Service:**
**IN U.S.A.:** P.O. Box 1341, Buffalo, NY 14240-8531
**IN CANADA:** P.O. Box 603, Fort Erie, Ontario L2A 5X3

**Want to try 2 free books from another series?** Call 1-800-873-8635 or visit www.ReaderService.com.

*Terms and prices subject to change without notice. Prices do not include sales taxes, which will be charged (if applicable) based on your state or country of residence. Canadian residents will be charged applicable taxes. Offer not valid in Quebec. This offer is limited to one order per household. Books received may not be as shown. Not valid for current subscribers to the Harlequin Historical or Harlequin Romance series. All orders subject to approval. Credit or debit balances in a customer's account(s) may be offset by any other outstanding balance owed by or to the customer. Please allow 4 to 6 weeks for delivery. Offer available while quantities last.

**Your Privacy**—Your information is being collected by Harlequin Enterprises ULC, operating as Harlequin Reader Service. For a complete summary of the information we collect, how we use this information and to whom it is disclosed, please visit our privacy notice located at corporate.harlequin.com/privacy-notice. From time to time we may also exchange your personal information with reputable third parties. If you wish to opt out of this sharing of your personal information, please visit readerservice.com/consumerschoice or call 1-800-873-8635. **Notice to California Residents**—Under California law, you have specific rights to control and access your data. For more information on these rights and how to exercise them, visit corporate.harlequin.com/california-privacy.

HHHRLP22

# Get 4 FREE REWARDS!

**We'll send you 2 FREE Books plus 2 FREE Mystery Gifts.**

**FREE**
Value Over
**$20**

Both the **Harlequin Intrigue®** and **Harlequin® Romantic Suspense** series feature compelling novels filled with heart-racing action-packed romance that will keep you on the edge of your seat.

---

**YES!** Please send me 2 FREE novels from the Harlequin Intrigue or Harlequin Romantic Suspense series and my 2 FREE gifts (gifts are worth about $10 retail). After receiving them, if I don't wish to receive any more books, I can return the shipping statement marked "cancel." If I don't cancel, I will receive 6 brand-new Harlequin Intrigue Larger-Print books every month and be billed just $5.99 each in the U.S. or $6.49 each in Canada, a savings of at least 14% off the cover price or 4 brand-new Harlequin Romantic Suspense books every month and be billed just $4.99 each in the U.S. or $5.74 each in Canada, a savings of at least 13% off the cover price. It's quite a bargain! Shipping and handling is just 50¢ per book in the U.S. and $1.25 per book in Canada.* I understand that accepting the 2 free books and gifts places me under no obligation to buy anything. I can always return a shipment and cancel at any time. The free books and gifts are mine to keep no matter what I decide.

Choose one: ☐ **Harlequin Intrigue**
 **Larger-Print**
 (199/399 HDN GNXC)

☐ **Harlequin Romantic Suspense**
 (240/340 HDN GNMZ)

Name (please print)

Address                                                                                    Apt. #

City                                    State/Province                        Zip/Postal Code

**Email:** Please check this box ☐ if you would like to receive newsletters and promotional emails from Harlequin Enterprises ULC and its affiliates. You can unsubscribe anytime.

### Mail to the **Harlequin Reader Service:**
**IN U.S.A.:** P.O. Box 1341, Buffalo, NY 14240-8531
**IN CANADA:** P.O. Box 603, Fort Erie, Ontario L2A 5X3

**Want to try 2 free books from another series?** Call 1-800-873-8635 or visit www.ReaderService.com.

---

# Visit
# ReaderService.com
# Today!

## As a valued member of the Harlequin Reader Service, you'll find these benefits and more at ReaderService.com:

- Try 2 free books from any series
- Access risk-free special offers
- View your account history & manage payments
- Browse the latest Bonus Bucks catalog

**Don't miss out!**

If you want to stay up-to-date on the latest at the Harlequin Reader Service and enjoy more content, make sure you've signed up for our monthly News & Notes email newsletter. Sign up online at ReaderService.com or by calling Customer Service at 1-800-873-8635.